SHEIKH
IN THE CITY

BY
JACKIE BRAUN

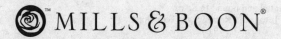

MILLS & BOON®

All the characters in this book have no existence outside the imagination of the author, and have no relation whatsoever to anyone bearing the same name or names. They are not even distantly inspired by any individual known or unknown to the author, and all the incidents are pure invention.

First published in Great Britain 2010
Harlequin Mills & Boon Limited,
Eton House, 18-24 Paradise Road, Richmond, Surrey TW9 1SR

© Jackie Braun Fridline 2010

ISBN: 978 0 263 87339 9

Harlequin Mills & Boon policy is to use papers that are natural, renewable and recyclable products and made from wood grown in sustainable forests. The logging and manufacturing process conform to the legal environmental regulations of the country of origin.

Printed and bound in Spain
by Litografia Rosés, S.A., Barcelona

and masc... ...off a pair of enigmatic brown eyes. His hair was the color of onyx, cut short enough to be respectable, but still long enough to make a woman's fingers itch to weave through it.

That was when Dan offered a smile that was every bit as warm as his hand had been. Forget the sauté—her temperature was reaching broiler status.

Dear Reader

I have a confession to make. When I decided to write SHEIKH IN THE CITY I was a little nervous. I'd never written a story about a sheikh. For that matter, I'd never created an entirely fictional country. But I was excited about the challenge.

Along the way I discovered the same thing my hero and heroine ultimately do: no matter the titles, customs or cultures, it all comes down to love.

Madani Tarim isn't only a sheikh. He's a man who falls in love with one woman despite his parents' plan for him to wed another. Both he and Emily Merit have to decide if their love is big enough to compensate for what they must give up to be together.

I hope you enjoy this special story.

Best wishes

Jackie Braun

Jackie Braun is a three-time RITA® Award finalist, a four-time National Readers' Choice Award finalist, and a past winner of the Rising Star Award. She worked for nearly two decades as an award-winning journalist, before leaving her full-time job to write fiction. She lives in mid-Michigan with her husband and their two sons. She loves to hear from readers and can be reached through her website at www.jackiebraun.com.

'Emily Merit gets her man in the end, but I still feel bad for saddling her with such a horrid younger sibling. If I'd treated my three older sisters a tenth as rotten, I wouldn't have survived childhood.'
—**Jackie Braun**

For "the greats":
Madison, Timmy and Morgan Kaiser;
Nathan and Brandon Tedder; and Brady Fridline.

CHAPTER ONE

"I THINK I've finally figured out who the guest of honor is," Arlene Williams said from the kitchen door, where she was peeking into the Hendersons' well-appointed dining room.

Babs and Denby Henderson regularly entertained powerful lawmakers, renowned academics, award-winning playwrights and European nobility at their Park Avenue soirées. Emily Merit, who'd been their caterer of choice for the past five years, didn't doubt tonight's guest of honor was any less impressive.

"Well, don't keep me in suspense," she replied, tongue-in-cheek, as she plated the evening's desserts.

Her sous chef shot her a black look before

saying, "I think he might be the hunky model in those underwear ads."

Emily glanced up at that. "The ones that are plastered all over the city's bus stops and subway stations?"

"And you claim to have sworn off men." Arlene grinned.

"I have, but those ads are impossible to miss."

Arlene peeked out again and her tone turned thoughtful. "Or he could be the actor who plays the CIA operative on *Restless Nights*. They both have that same sensual mouth."

Emily rolled her eyes. Where she'd sworn off men, she couldn't keep track of the number of guys Arlene had drooled over in the past month alone. "Get away from the door already and give me a hand with dessert."

"Uh-oh. He's…he's coming this way."

Emily frowned. Great. Just what she needed, an audience. She didn't like people in her kitchen when she worked, especially if they were only coming in to flirt with her assistant. Technically this wasn't Emily's kitchen, but the same principle applied.

"He's with Mrs. Henderson," Arlene added and let the door swing fully closed.

Emily relaxed a little upon hearing that. She figured she knew why they were coming to the kitchen. She'd met Babs five years earlier through her then-boyfriend, Reed, who had a business relationship with Bab's husband, Denby. One day when a catering company left the Hendersons in the lurch just hours before a dinner party, Reed had volunteered Emily's services. At the time, she was just out of culinary school and her only catering jobs had been casual gatherings for family and friends. She'd been scared to death, to put it mildly. But her cooking that evening was a huge hit, and the Hendersons proved to be the launching pad for her career.

As a client, Babs could be flighty and trying, but she knew lots of people whose pockets were every bit as deep as her own and—bless her—she'd made it her mission to introduce them to Emily. Thanks in part to the Henderson's patronage Emily had been able to renovate the kitchen in her otherwise modest East Village apartment without dipping into her savings for the restaurant she dreamed of opening one day.

The older woman was probably bringing her guest in for an introduction. In Emily's book the title of potential client was more important than what he did for a living, even if he really was the hunky model with the ripped abs and buff biceps in those underwear ads.

Arlene hoisted the tray of desserts, leaving the kitchen just before Babs swept in with the mystery man. The older woman wore vintage Dior and was doused in her usual Chanel. Her high-piled hair prevented Emily from getting a good look at Mr. Hunky.

"Emily, my dear, you outdid yourself this evening," Babs proclaimed in her usual dramatic fashion. Her smile sparkled as brightly as the large diamond pendant hanging low in her décolletage. "All of my guests are raving about the herb-crusted salmon." She turned and tucked her hand into the crook of the man's arm then, drawing him to her side. "And that includes my very special guest, Sh—"

"Please, call me Dan," he inserted.

He wasn't the underwear model, but

Emily's mouth dropped open anyway. She couldn't fault her assistant for standing at the door half the evening gawking. God, he was gorgeous. Drop-dead so. The monosyllabic name, however, didn't suit him. It was too simple, too... Western.

Which was why she frowned and said, "Dan?"

"It is what you would call a nickname." His words were adorned with an accent she couldn't quite place, but its effect was potent. It had her hormones threatening to snap and sizzle like vegetables sautéing in hot oil. It bothered her that she wasn't completely immune. She wanted to be. God knew, after what had happened with Reed, she should be.

The man was saying, "I find that when I travel in your country it is easier for some people to pronounce than my given name."

That made sense, she supposed. Still, he didn't look like a Dan. Nor did he resemble the underwear model Arlene mistook him for, though he certainly had the body for it. He was tall with a lean, athletic build that accentuated the clean lines of the expertly tailored suit he wore. His face, however, was more angular and masculine than the male model in question, and slashes of dark brow set off a pair of enigmatic brown eyes. His hair was the color of onyx and cut short enough to be respectable, but still long enough to make a woman's fingers itch to weave through it.

She stretched out her hand, but only to shake his. "I'm Emily Merit."

His palm was warm against hers, his grasp light but not as condescendingly loose as some men's could be. She found it easier to concentrate on his grip than the bizarre reaction her body was having to the benign contact. It now felt as if her sizzling hormones had been placed under the broiler.

When the handshake ended, Emily smoothed down the front of her mannish chef coat. Normally she wasn't vain, but his physical perfection made her painfully aware that her hair was pulled back in a severe, net-covered chignon and what little makeup she'd applied that morning most likely had worn off.

Babs spoke up then. "As I told you earlier, *Dan,* Mr. Henderson and I wouldn't dream of letting anyone else cater our gatherings. As far as we're concerned, she's the best in Manhattan."

Dan nodded and offered a smile that was every bit as warm as his hand had been. Forget broiler, her temperature was reaching kiln status. "Then I must have her."

Was he aware of the double entendre? His bland expression made it difficult to be sure. Emily certainly was. Before she could stop herself, she sputtered ridiculously, "But I…I don't even know your last name."

"Allow me to remedy that. It's Tarim." His expression was no longer bland. The corners of his mouth turned up and laughter lit his dark eyes. He was amused. Definitely.

Emily wasn't since it came at her expense. God, what was wrong with her? This was completely out of character, not to mention unprofessional. Though it shouldn't have been necessary, she reminded herself that she was a respected and sought-after chef who had graduated from one of the country's best culinary schools. She wasn't some silly schoolgirl conversing with the football team's star quarterback.

Babs cleared her throat. "Well, if the two of you will excuse me, I should get back to the party. Promise me you won't keep him occupied for too long, Emily. My other guests are eager to spend more time with him."

"I'll shoo him out as soon as possible," she said with a tight smile. She meant it, too. She planned to get down to business and then usher him out. As soon as they were alone, she said, "So, what can I do for you, Mr. Tarim?"

"Dan, please. And may I call you Emily?"

"By all means." Her name, which she'd always considered plain and old-fashioned, sounded almost exotic when he said it.

"I'm planning a small dinner party before I leave Manhattan. I would like to repay the generosity of those who have hosted me during my stay."

"Is this your first time in the city?" she inquired politely, even as she sneaked a glance at her watch.

"No. I am here several times a year for

business purposes mainly. In the past, I've used the services of someone else to cater my parties, but the meal you prepared tonight has caused me to change my mind."

"Thank you. I'm flattered."

And she was. His clothes screamed expensive, which meant he could afford to hire any catering company he wanted. She wondered which one he'd used, though she didn't ask him. She'd discreetly inquire later. It was good to know who her competition was. Good for business and, depending on the caterer, good for her ego. For the past several years, she had slaved and sacrificed to build a client base and solidify her reputation for high quality. Knowing that those efforts had paid off also made it easier to accept their high cost to her personal life.

She thought of Reed then. They'd dated six years. Everyone, including Emily, had assumed they would wed eventually. Looking back now, though, she could see the cracks that had only gotten deeper and wider as she'd pursued her dreams. When catering had been a hobby or merely a part-time job, he'd seemed proud of her. When it turned into a real career, pulling in serious money and creating enough buzz to land Emily a mention in The *New York Times*, his enthusiasm had cooled considerably. When she began to dream about opening a restaurant, he'd done his best to talk her out of it, quoting statistics on the number of establishments that failed each year. Finally he'd found someone else: Emily's sister.

"The guest list will be small, no more than six guests and myself," Dan was saying, pulling Emily back to the present.

"When were you thinking?" she asked, mentally flipping through her appointment calendar.

"The Saturday after next. The notice is short, I know." His expression held an apology. "As I said, I usually hire someone else to handle my dinner parties. But I'm hoping you will find room in your schedule for me. As my gracious hostess said, you *are* the best."

His lips twitched charmingly, but this time, immersed in the details of business, she was able to ignore the pyre of heat.

* * *

Dan, also known as Sheikh Madani Abdul Tarim, wasn't one to settle for anything but the best. Thanks to his position and wealth, he'd never had to. Still, he didn't consider himself demanding so much as discerning. Tonight's meal was first-rate. He had to admit, though, he hadn't expected the chef who'd created it to be quite so young.

Or so attractive.

Even wearing mannish attire and with her hair scraped back in that hideous fashion there was no denying the tug of male interest he felt. Of course, he wouldn't act on it. With the official announcement of his engagement fast approaching, he wasn't in the market for a relationship, casual or otherwise. Still, Emily Merit almost made him wish his future hadn't been decided when he was still a toddler.

He blamed it on her eyes. They were a rich combination of blues and greens, and reminded him of the Mediterranean Sea near his family's summer home. Her gaze was direct and assessing, making it clear that she considered herself his equal.

He liked that. As it was, his title and

position intimidated too many people—
male and female. Perhaps that was why he
hadn't allowed the hostess to formally introduce him. And why he had decided to
tell Emily Merit his name was merely Dan.
He preferred anonymity every now and
then, if only to keep himself grounded. As
his father often told him, when he became
ruler of Kashaqra, Madani would need to
look out for the interests of all of the
country's people.

That didn't mean he didn't prefer to get his
way. So, he prodded, "Well?"

"Unfortunately I'm booked to make the
meal and cake for a child's fifth birthday
celebration that day."

It didn't seem like a huge obligation to
him. "Will it take all day?"

"In most instances, it wouldn't." Her
tone turned wry. "But this particular party
is an hour outside the city in Connecticut
and the parents are insisting on an epicurean feast."

"You don't agree with their menu choices,"
he gathered.

She sobered and said diplomatically, "It's

not my place to agree or disagree with a client's menu choices."

"But?" Raising his eyebrows he invited her confidence.

After a moment she admitted, "I just don't think the average kindergartner will enjoy what they have selected. After all, certain foods are considered an *acquired* taste for good reason."

Madani found himself chuckling, charmed by her honesty. "What have they ordered? Caviar blintzes?"

"Close." She smiled and he spied a dimple lurking low on her right cheek. It lent an air of impishness to her otherwise classical features. "At least I managed to talk the mother out of an appetizer of duck liver pâté in favor of ham rolls. Even so, I'm pretty sure there are going to be plenty of leftovers. She wouldn't budge on the veal marsala or the side of roasted root vegetables."

"I guess this means you won't be available."

She nibbled her lower lip. The gesture was uncomfortably and unaccountably sexy. "I may be able to accommodate you," she said at last. "I have an assistant I could leave in charge of the birthday party. Of course, a lot depends on the time of your gathering and what you would like to serve."

Madani wasn't sure if his relief came from knowing Emily would be preparing the meal for his guests or from knowing he would have the opportunity to see her again. "I can be very amenable when the situation calls for it. When shall we meet to discuss the details?"

"I'm free tomorrow morning if you are."

He had three meetings lined up back-to-back before noon, but he nodded anyway. As he'd said, he could be amenable when the situation called for it. This one did, though he refused to explore why he felt that way.

Emily went to retrieve a business card. Handing it to him, she said, "I'm an early riser. Feel free to call any time after nine o'clock."

The card was still in Madani's hand and a smile on his face when he met his driver downstairs.

"I trust you had a good evening," Azeem Harrah said.

Azeem was not only Madani's driver, but

a trusted confidant and sometimes body-guard who traveled with him whenever he went abroad. The two men had been friends since boyhood. Azeem's father was a long-serving member of Kashaqra's parliament. His uncle sat on the country's high court. He was educated and at times outspoken, but above all he was loyal—to Madani and to Kashaqra.

"Very good. The Hendersons are generous hosts and the food was…exquisite." His smile broadened.

"I know that smile." Azeem laughed as he shifted the Mercedes into Drive and eased the vehicle into traffic. "A woman is behind it."

Madani grew serious. "You are mistaken, my friend."

"Am I?"

"Those days are over."

"Why?" Azeem challenged.

"You know why, even if you do not agree with my decision," he said.

"That is because it was *not* your decision," Azeem shot back. "I cannot believe you are going through with an arranged marriage. You!"

In Kashaqra, Madani was known for holding much more progressive views than his father, even though during the past three decades Sheikh Adil Hammad Tarim had ushered in much change.

"You know my reasons."

"Your father's health is fine, *sadiqi*," Azeem said, using the Arabic word for friend. "The heart attack he suffered last fall was mild."

It hadn't seemed mild at the time. Madani closed his eyes, recalling anew the way his father's face had turned ashen just before he'd crumpled to the floor. They'd been arguing over this very matter. Arranged marriages were not set in stone. They could be nullified under a limited set of circumstances, none of which applied to Madani. Still, given Adil's position, he could have voided it, but his father wouldn't hear of it. His own union had been contracted and all had turned out well. He believed the same would hold true for his son.

"My engagement to Nawar is his wish, his will."

Azeem shook his head. He didn't understand. Madani didn't expect him to.

"Well, you are not engaged yet. There would be nothing wrong with a final...*fling,* I believe is the word the Americans use."

Madani gazed out the car's tinted window and let the conversation lapse. He wasn't officially engaged. That much was true. His betrothal to Nawar would be announced later in the summer. But he was not free. Indeed, in this regard, he never had been.

Emily arrived home just before midnight. She felt exhausted and invigorated at the same time. In addition to the enigmatic Dan, two other guests of the Hendersons' party had requested her business cards tonight. As it was, the Hendersons had paid her generously, per usual. Of course, she'd had to hire a couple of extra hands to pull off the meal and serving, but deducting for expenses, wages and other incidentals, she still had a decent sum to deposit into her savings account come Monday morning.

It took her three trips to cart everything from the catering van to her fourth-floor apartment from which she also ran her business. Then she had to move the van to her spot at a paid lot half a block away. Once in her apartment she wanted to collapse on the couch, but she spent another twenty minutes putting away chafing dishes, serving utensils and other items before she finally propped her aching feet atop the coffee table in what passed for a living room.

The stack of mail cushioning her heels drew her attention. She hadn't had time for more than a cursory glance at the envelopes before leaving for the Hendersons that afternoon. Most contained bills. A few were junk mail. Only one was personal and would require a response. She pulled her feet to the floor and sifted through the pile until she found it. Even without opening the thick envelope she knew what was inside: an invitation to her younger sister's wedding.

On an oath, she ripped back the flap and pulled out a square of ivory vellum. The quality of the paper and the engraved lettering had cost their parents a fortune, but then nothing was ever too good for Elle.

Emily's younger sister could do no wrong. Even the fact that she was engaged to marry Emily's ex-boyfriend, who had not yet been an ex when Elle first began seeing him, elicited no censure from their parents. Rather, Emily had been called on to be more "understanding" and, later, to be "happy" that her flighty baby sibling was finally settling down.

Elle Lauren Merit and Reed David Benedict, together with their parents, request the honor of your presence at their wedding…

Emily got no further than that before crumpling the invitation in her hand. Out of respect for the tree that had been chopped down to produce the paper, she decided to toss it in the recycling bin rather than the garbage. But she had no intention of *honoring* Elle and Reed with her presence as they exchanged I Dos, any more than she planned to give in to her mother's urging that she don a bridesmaid gown and join the wedding party.

It wasn't that Emily couldn't forgive them. She wanted to believe she was bigger than that despite their monumental betrayal. No, it was the fact that neither of them had ever so much as acknowledged the pain they'd caused her or offered an apology of any sort.

Quite the opposite. Elle had manipulated her illicit affair with her older sister's longtime beau into proof positive that true love could not be denied.

"It's destiny, Em. The answer to my prayers. Reed and I were made for one another," she'd had the gall to claim. As if Emily was supposed to feel so much better knowing her sister had been hot for her boy-friend from the very beginning.

Reed had been neither romantic nor idyllic. Rather, he shifted the blame for his infidelity squarely to Emily.

"If you weren't always so busy catering parties you might have noticed how unhappy I was," he'd told her when she'd learned of the affair.

His remark had landed like a sucker punch. "I have a business, Reed." A business he'd been only too happy to help her create and grow when it had been convenient for him.

"Don't remind me." He'd snorted in disgust. "You're very much in demand these days."

"Am I supposed to apologize for being successful?"

"No, but you shouldn't act so surprised

that with so much free time on my hands I found someone else."

"That someone else is my sister!" she'd shouted.

He'd merely shrugged. "Elle understands me. She's not interested in having a demanding career and working long hours. She wants to be supportive of me so that I can advance in mine."

Gaping at him, Emily wondered if Reed had always been so chauvinistic or if her growing success had brought it out. Regardless, his attitude had her blood boiling.

"So, women can't have a demanding job or pursue their dreams without expecting the men they're involved with to stray. Is that what you're saying?"

"I'm saying no man wants to place second to a woman's ambitions."

While Reed clearly felt a woman should be thrilled to place second to a man's, his parting shot contained enough truth that Emily had decided if she was only entitled to one true love, it was safer for her heart to choose cooking.

Sighing now, Emily rose and, peeling off

her stained chef's coat, headed in the direction of the bedroom that, a year ago—a lifetime ago—she'd shared with the man who would soon make her sister his wife.

CHAPTER TWO

EVEN though she had retired late, Emily rose just before eight o'clock, as was her practice. She was a morning person, even though these days her career often demanded late nights. Caffeine—and lots of it—helped her stay on her feet.

Her East Village apartment measured barely seven hundred square feet and offered an uninspiring view of the alley from its two hazy, south-facing windows. In addition to the one small bedroom where she'd passed the night, it contained a hopelessly outdated bathroom and a cramped living room that doubled as her business office. Its kitchen, however, was a work of art.

When she and Reed had moved in a few years earlier, splitting the down payment and monthly expenses, the kitchen had been horrendous while the other rooms hadn't been quite as space-challenged. The major renovation she'd treated herself to after he'd packed up his belongings and gone was responsible for that. As far as trades went, Emily figured she'd come out way ahead.

Gone was the galley that had barely allowed room for an under-counter refrigerator and persnickety electric stove. A wall had been knocked out, new wiring and plumbing installed. The new kitchen, which took up the space of the other three rooms combined, had a multi-burner gas cooktop, double ovens and a commercial grade refrigerator. It also offered plenty of counter space for food preparation and ample storage for her extensive collection of pots, pans, gadgets and appliances.

At this point in Emily's life, her surroundings reflected her priorities perfectly, and she would make no apologies for that.

One of the perks of working from home was that her morning commute could be accomplished in a dozen steps while wearing her pajamas. Emily was seated at her computer, tweaking the ingredients in a recipe for roast duck, when she heard a knock at the door. A glance through the peephole had her cursing.

It was Dan.

He appeared freshly shaved and was wearing a tie. Despite the limited view, she was sure he looked every bit as polished and sophisticated as he had when she'd met him at the Hendersons' the evening before. Meanwhile, she was clad in wrinkled draw-string pants and a snug white T-shirt that couldn't camouflage the fact that she wasn't wearing a bra. God only knew what her hair was doing.

To think she'd been concerned about her appearance last night! When she'd told him to call, she should have been more clear that she meant on the phone. And why, she wondered now, had she ever thought it a good idea to put her address on her business card?

Emily debated not answering his knock. She could get his number from Babs and contact him later in the day. But what if she couldn't? What if she failed to reach him and he decided not to hire her despite the interest he'd expressed the prior evening?

Okay, she had an overactive imagination, but this much she knew: It never paid to be rude to a client.

So, after running her fingers through her hair in the hope of taming it, she flipped the dead bolt and unlatched the security chain. As she opened the door, she maneuvered her body behind it, using it as a shield so that only her head and one shoulder were visible. Pasting a bright smile on her face, she offered a greeting.

"Dan. Hello. This is a surprise."

"Good morning." His voice was as rich as the freshly ground roasted Kona beans in her coffeemaker, but his engaging expression faltered almost immediately. "You weren't expecting me."

"No." She let out a self-conscious laugh. "Or is that yes?" When his frown deepened she clarified, "You're right. I wasn't expecting you. Sorry."

"But I thought we had agreed to this morning? I believe you said I could call on you any time after nine."

"Yes." She coughed delicately. *"Call."*

He closed his eyes, grimaced. "You

expected me to *telephone*. My profuse
apologies for the intrusion. I will *telephone*
you later."

He dipped his head and stepped backward.
She doubted he often found himself lost in
translation, even if English wasn't his first
language. His show of embarrassment
helped to chase away some of Emily's. As
he turned to leave, she put a hand on his arm
to stop him.

"Don't go. You're here now and I'm free.
Just give me a few minutes to dress."

Despite the invitation, he hesitated at the
threshold. "Are you certain? We can resched-
ule our meeting. I have no wish to inconvenience you."

A man who didn't wish to inconvenience
her. *Are you married?* The ridiculous
question wanted to slip from her lips. Instead
Emily waved her free hand and said,
"Nonsense. Please, come in."

Modesty, however, had her turning away
without waiting to see if Dan actually did so.
Even before she heard the apartment door
close, she was in her bedroom, a battered
oak six-panel between them as she rooted

through the contents of her jammed closet for something presentable to wear.

As the eldest child and only son of his country's ruler, as well as the president of what was becoming a thriving export business, Madani often traveled to the United States from his native Kashaqra. Thanks in part to his schooling, first at Harvard and later Oxford, he was fluent in seven languages, one of them English. When he'd told Emily Merit he would call in the morning, he should have been clearer. But he hadn't figured it would matter one way or another. How was he to know that the address listed on her business card was her home? Or that she would answer the door in her night-clothes looking sexy and sleep tousled?

As it was, when he'd awoken that morning she'd been on his mind. Now, after watching thin cotton cling to her curves while she'd hustled away, he had the uncomfortable feeling she was going to be a blight on his concentration for the entire day.

He should go. Blaming curiosity, he stepped inside the apartment instead.

The small living room opened into a surprisingly large kitchen. It was a chef's dream, he supposed, noting the double ovens on the far wall and the multiburnered, stainless steel stove. As for the array of gadgets on the countertop, other than the coffeemaker he was clueless to their use. While he enjoyed eating a good meal, he'd never prepared one.

Overall, the entire space wasn't as big as the smallest bedroom in the tower suite he maintained at The Mark for his frequent visits to the city, but she'd made good use of every inch. Sleek cabinetry ran the full height of the walls in the kitchen, and in the living area her computer and printer were tucked inside an armoire. The doors were open now, revealing a chocolate soufflé screen saver and a plethora of notes pinned to the corkboard that lined the interior of the doors.

She'd cleverly used stacks of cookbooks to form the base of a coffee table, over which was placed an oval of glass. The slip-covered sofa behind it was the room's only nod to comfort, but it was the brightly hued throw on the back of it that caught his attention. He recognized the craftsmanship and the centuries' old pattern. It came from his homeland.

"Would you care for some coffee?"

He turned at the sound of her voice. "Yes, thank you."

He followed her into the kitchen, where she poured him a cup and topped off her own.

"Cream or sugar?" she asked.

"Black is fine." He'd acquired a taste for Western coffee, though he preferred the sweetened variety of his country.

She'd pulled her chestnut hair into a softer-looking version of the style she'd worn the night before, minus the net, of course. For a moment he wished she'd left it loose as it had been when he'd arrived. He liked the way it had waved in defiance around her face before falling just past her shoulders. The pink blouse she wore wrapped at the waist, accentuating its smallness. Her trousers were tan and mannish in style, but the flair of her hips and the tips of a lethal-looking pair of pumps that peeked out from the cuffed hem kept the cut from appearing too masculine.

When he realized he was staring, he glanced away. "You have an impressive kitchen."

"Thanks. I like it."

"Was it recently renovated?"

"Less than a year ago." Something in her expression changed and her chin rose fractionally, as if in challenge. "My business is growing, so I decided to go all out. Besides, I spend most of my time in here whether I'm working for a client or just puttering for fun."

She sat on one of the stools lined up next to the island. He took the one next to hers and swiveled so he could face her.

"You cook for fun?"

"I'm afraid I can't help myself. I absolutely adore food."

His gaze skimmed over her, lingering on her slender waist. "And yet you are…small."

She laughed outright at what he realized too late was a rude observation for a man to make. Wincing, he said, "I shouldn't have said that. Sorry."

"Oh, no. Don't apologize." She laid a hand on his arm. "I can't think of a woman alive who doesn't like to be told she's not fat."

He felt his face grow warm. This made

twice since arriving on Emily's doorstep that he'd embarrassed himself. He didn't care for the sensation. Indeed, he wasn't used to putting his foot in his mouth, especially where women were concerned. But the amusement shimmering in her blue eyes took away some of his chagrin.

"I only make that observation because a lot of the chefs I know are…more substantially proportioned," he said, trying for diplomacy.

She sighed. "Unfortunately that's a hazard of the profession. All those little tastes can add up over time."

"How have you managed to avoid it?"

"Exercise and nervous energy." At his frown she clarified, "I have a gym membership. I try to work out at least three times a week. The rest of the time I fret and pace, or so my assistant tells me."

Fret and pace? She seemed too confident for either. "Have you been in business for long?"

"Why do you ask? Are you having second thoughts about hiring me?" Amusement shimmered in her eyes again.

"No. Once I make a commitment I keep it."

"But you haven't committed. No contract has been signed," she reminded him lightly.

Madani thought of Nawar, his bride-to-be in Kashaqra, and of the long-held agreement between their families. No contract had been signed for that, either. But it was understood. It had always been understood. "Sometimes one's word is enough."

"I prefer a signature," she replied. "No offense. I just find it easier to do business that way since not everyone's word tends to be equal."

"True." He nodded, thinking of the deals he would finalize later that day. "Legally speaking, it's always best to have documentation. I run an export business… among other things."

"May I ask you a question?" At his nod, Emily went on. "Your accent, I can't quite place it."

"I am from Kashaqra." He thought of his homeland now, missing it since he'd been gone a month already. It was bounded by mountains on one side and a swath of desert on the other. Due to his father's foresight and diligence, it had avoided the unrest that had plagued some of the other countries in the region. It was Madani's goal to continue that tradition. It was also his goal to see the export business he'd started continue to grow so his people could prosper.

Her brows wrinkled. "Geography wasn't one of my better subjects, but that's in the Middle East, I believe."

"Yes. Near Saudi Arabia. Even though we lack our good neighbor's oil riches, we are wealthy in other ways."

"How so?"

"Our artisans are unrivaled."

"In your humble opinion." She grinned and he caught the wink of that solitaire dimple.

Madani smiled in return, but meant it when he said, "I do not believe in being humble when it comes to praising the work of my countrymen. Indeed, it is my hope that eventually, in addition to finding markets for it abroad, it will entice tourists to come and visit our country."

"You make me eager to see their work for myself."

"You already have and obviously are a fan." At her surprised expression, he pointed to the sofa. "That throw was hand woven in a little village called Sakala. The pattern dates back seven hundred years and has been passed down from generation to generation. Mothers make it for their daughters when they are to wed. It is said to bring good luck to the union."

Her expression turned surprisingly cool. "Maybe I should give it to my sister."

"Your sister is to be married?"

"Yes." She sipped her coffee and changed the subject. "I had no idea that throw enjoyed such a rich history when I saw it hanging in the window of an eclectic little shop not far from here."

"Salim's Treasures," he guessed. The owner's wife had family in Kashaqra.

"Yeah, that's the one. I paid a small fortune for it," she admitted. "But I had to have it. The colors are so rich and vibrant."

"Vibrant." He nodded, but his gaze was on her.

The moment stretched before she glanced away. Was she embarrassed? Flattered? Should he apologize?

"We should get down to business," she said, ending the silence. "About your dinner party, did you have a type of cuisine in mind?"

Emily couldn't help being in good spirits after Dan Tarim left her apartment later that morning. It had nothing to do with the man, she assured herself, though she found him extremely sexy with his dark good looks and fathomless eyes. Rather, it was because she'd landed another catering job that, after deducting expenses and incidentals, would allow her to deposit a sizable chunk of money into her savings account. The man obviously didn't believe in doing anything halfway.

She felt the same when it came to her restaurant, which she planned to call The Merit. It was inching closer to reality by the day. Another year or so and she would be able to approach the bank with her business plan. Given the number of restaurants that failed each year, even in a good economy, Emily knew she would have to show the bank why she was a good risk.

She could picture the place so clearly. The

menus would be leather bound and tasseled. The tables would sport crisp white linens and be topped with candles to add an air of intimacy and romance when the lights were turned low. But the bow to convention would end there. The food would be eclectic and bold, a smattering of tastes from around the globe all given her signature twist. As such she felt the best location for it was somewhere in the Village.

Her thoughts returned to Dan. At the end of their meeting, she'd promised to work up menu selections for his approval by the end of the week. He'd been open to suggestions, which made him the kind of client she preferred, since that allowed her to be creative. He'd made only one request, one she would have no problem honoring since he was footing the bill. He had a fondness for white truffles and insisted at least one dish include them.

The Italian delicacy went for up to ten thousand dollars a pound, which was why Emily rarely cooked with it. Even the Hendersons, who were exceedingly generous when it came to trying to please their guests' discerning palates, had never requested a recipe that included the pricey tuber.

"I'm in heaven." Emily sighed as she lugged a stack of books holding her favorite recipes to the kitchen's island.

It only took the phone to ring for her to return to earth. Then, as soon as Emily heard her mother's voice, she descended a bit further south.

"My goodness but you've been hard to get in touch with lately," Miranda complained by way of a greeting.

Since her mother had forgone social niceties, Emily decided to as well. "Have I?"

"You know you have. You can try to avoid me, but you can't avoid the fact that your sister is getting married in August."

The M word landed like a bomb, obliterating what remained of Emily's good mood.

"I'm not avoiding it, Mom." The reply came out clipped, despite Emily's best efforts to sound blasé.

"I know this is hard for you, but it's really for the best in the long-term. He and Elle are so much better suited than the two of you were. When are you going to forgive them?"

When they ask me to, she thought.

"On their silver wedding anniversary?" her mother went on dramatically.

"That's optimistic," Emily muttered.

"You need to be a bigger person. Your sister is so happy and content. Your father and I have never seen Elle like this. It's what we've been hoping for for years. Can't you be happy for her?"

Guilt niggled. Her mother was good at planting the seed and then helping it grow. Miranda had been nurturing this particular one since Elle first flashed an engagement ring.

"I really do have to go, Mom."

"Elle's bridal shower is next Sunday."

"You know I can't come. As I've told you half a dozen times already, I'm booked that day." It was a lie. She had that particular Sunday free.

"Please try. For the sake of family harmony."

Emily hung up wondering why she was the only one expected to carry that load.

Dan flipped his cell phone closed on an oath as Azeem maneuvered the Mercedes through

Manhattan traffic. This message, like the one before it, was from his mother. Given the time difference between New York and Kashaqra, Fadilah must consider the matter to be vitally important. That meant he couldn't avoid calling her back much longer.

"Is everything all right?" Azeem asked. "Your father?"

"Is well." Fadilah would not have been so vague if that were the case. "My mother says she *needs* to speak with me," he said wryly, knowing that would explain it all.

Azeem nodded. "She is the only woman I know who can make you squirm. But not for long, *sadiqi*. If you insist on going through with the wedding, Nawar will enjoy that right as well."

Though the words were offered in jest, the challenge was unmistakable.

"Drop me off at the next light," he said.

"But Mayhew's is at Fifth Avenue and Forty-Third," Azeem reminded him.

"I know. I want to walk the rest of the way." When his friend frowned, he added, "This is the first warm, sunny day we've had in nearly a week. I want to take advantage of it."

"As you wish." But Azeem's expression said he wasn't buying the explanation.

Madani glanced at his watch after the Mercedes drove away. It wasn't quite noon, which meant he still had forty minutes before his rescheduled appointment with a potential distributor. He started walking, his pace slow and leisurely. Even with heat rising from the street, the temperature was pleasant and the humidity low after a week of thunderstorms, making him glad to be outdoors and moving under his own steam. In Kashaqra, even with all of the amenities his wealth and position afforded, Madani enjoyed walking. In addition to being good exercise, it gave a man time to think, plan and put things into perspective. He needed to do that now, he decided, his thoughts returning to the phone message.

His mother probably wanted to discuss the engagement announcement or, he swallowed thickly, his wedding. Just thinking about marriage had Madani tugging his necktie loose as he strode down the sidewalk. As his parents kept reminding him, it was the next logical step in his life. He was thirty-two, educated, well-traveled and established. The time had come for him to take a wife and start a family. As the next in line to rule the country, it also was Madani's duty.

Turning matrimony into an obligation hardly made it any more palatable.

Still, he shouldn't complain. Nawar, the bride his parents had chosen for him, was beautiful in both face and form. She also was bright, only recently finishing up her PhD in economics at Kashaqra's leading university. Per her request, all talk of marriage had been postponed until she had completed her education, causing Madani to wonder if her pursuit of a doctoral degree was an indication of her own mixed emotions.

Here in the West, arranged marriages were considered archaic and unromantic. Even in his country many of the younger generation considered such alliances old-fashioned and unnecessary. After all, shouldn't picking a life partner be left to the two people involved?

Azeem, who to Madani's knowledge wasn't even seriously involved with anyone, was surprisingly outspoken on the matter, which in turn made him annoyingly out-spoken in his dismay over Madani's decision to honor his arranged betrothal.

"You have an opportunity to lead even before taking your father's place," Azeem had hollered during one of their many arguments on the subject. "If you refuse to marry under these conditions, others would be willing to follow your example."

He'd considered that at one time, but he'd shaken his head. "It is done."

Madani hadn't just been referring to the fact that his betrothal to the daughter of one of his father's closest political allies had been arranged when he was still a toddler. As he'd told Azeem, it was his father's wish. What reason did he have to risk his father's health? Nawar would make a suitable wife. Besides, the notion of marrying for love seemed far-fetched. He'd spent time with plenty of women over the years, but he'd never felt the intense emotion the poets claimed existed.

For no reason he could fathom, his thoughts turned to Emily Merit.

"I was unaware you knew someone in this

part of Manhattan," Azeem had said when they'd arrived outside her apartment building that morning. "She must be very pretty to have roused you so early after a late night. Am I to conclude you have changed your mind about a final fling with which to remember your bachelorhood?"

"This is a business meeting," he'd answered irritably. "Nothing more."

It *was* a business matter, but the pretty young woman he'd hired to cater his dinner party also had captured his interest.

CHAPTER THREE

THE FOLLOWING week, Emily was still on Madani's mind, which he supposed made sense since his personal assistant had given him the list of the RSVPs for his dinner party. He decided to call her.

She answered on the fourth ring, sounding cheerful if breathless.

"Hello, Emily. This is Dan Tarim."

"Dan, hi. You must be psychic. I've been thinking about you and was just about to call."

Her laughter, light and musical, floated over the line. He pictured her face with its errant dimple, blue eyes and soft mouth. Interest, an uncomfortable portion of it sexual, gave a swift tug.

"You've been thinking about me?"

"Yes. I've put together the most amazing menu for your guests."

"Menu," he repeated.

"As I promised, I want to run it by you before I purchase all of the ingredients, especially those pricey white truffles. And, of course, I will need a head count."

"Of course." He cleared his throat. "That's actually the reason for my call. One of my guests and his wife will be out of town, leaving just two other couples and myself."

"That's too bad. I'll adjust the portions accordingly." Then, "You don't have a date?"

"A date?"

"I only ask because Babs Henderson insists on an even number at her gatherings. I've known her to ask her social secretary to sit in to avoid going odd."

"No. I don't have a date."

"Really?" She sounded surprised. "Okay."

"You think I should have one?"

"Well, no. It's not a requirement or anything. I just thought that someone who looks like you would have one if not several women…" She coughed, clearly embarrassed. "Um, never mind."

Manhattan was far from his homeland, but
Madani had spent enough time in the city
that he knew plenty of women he could
invite. Women who would drop everything
to spend an evening in his company, even
though he always made it clear, without
going into too much detail, that a long-term
relationship would never materialize.

He didn't feel he was being unfaithful to
Nawar. After all, they were not officially
engaged. In truth, they had met on only a
handful occasions during which he'd been
allowed no more than to brush both of her
cheeks with his lips in his culture's customary greeting.

He pushed thoughts of Nawar and all other
women away. All other women save Emily.

"When are you free to discuss the menu?"

"You want to meet?" She sounded surprised. "We can…or, if your schedule is full,
I can e-mail you the proposed menu and we
can go over it on the telephone."

"Is that how you normally conduct
business?"

"Sometimes." She laughed, the sound
again pleasing. "I've found that there's really

no such thing as normal. Some clients want to try samples of the dishes I suggest. Others leave everything to me. And then there are the high-maintenance types who demand they accompany me to the grocery store."

"And you let them?"

"I don't encourage it, but for what I charge…" She cleared her throat. "You're a businessman. The client is always right, remember?"

"Indeed."

"So?" she prodded.

"When can we meet? And, of course, I'll want samples." He chuckled before adding, "I may even request to come shopping with you. Those who know me well will tell you I can be very demanding."

"Are you serious?"

"On all counts." Though he hadn't been till she'd called him on it. "Are you free Saturday night?"

"I'm a caterer." Her tone was dry.

"Day then." Which was for the best, he reminded himself. Even in his country, Saturday night was the territory of couples and dates.

"I have a dinner party for twelve at seven o'clock. It's going to take up a lot of my time since my assistant has asked for the night off. I plan to start some of my prep work the night before."

"So the morning should find you free."

Her laughter was exasperated now. "You don't take no for an answer, do you?"

"No. The customer is always right, remember?"

"Absolutely. Come by anytime between ten and noon. I can't promise samples of the meal I'd like to make for your guests, but we can go over the menu and I'll be happy to answer any questions you have."

"Very good. Until then."

For no reason he could nail down, Madani was smiling when he hung up.

Dan arrived at Emily's door promptly at ten the following morning. This time, she was ready for him. She answered his knock fully dressed and coiffed, her teeth brushed and her makeup applied.

She'd taken a little more time on her appearance than she normally did on a day that would find her toiling in her kitchen, but she wanted to present a crisp and professional image since she had a client coming over. Of course, that didn't explain why she'd opted to forego a white, standard-issue chef's coat in favor of a short-sleeved teal blouse that brought out flecks of blue in her eyes. Thankfully, enough sanity prevailed that she'd layered an apron over the dry-clean-only fabric before starting to chop the ingredients for one of the three appetizers she was to prepare.

"Good morning." His voice was as deep and rich as she remembered.

"Good morning."

He was dressed casually in tan slacks, a pair of broken-in loafers and a white oxford shirt. He wore no tie, which made sense since it was Saturday. Even so he radiated the same authority and sophistication he did wearing expensive, tailored suits.

Realizing she'd been staring at him while he remained in the hallway, she backed up and invited him inside.

After Emily closed the door, she turned to find that he was staring, too. At her apron.

"You are already working?"

"For hours now. I've been up since six, although I didn't get anything accomplished until after I'd had a cup of espresso. I was up a little late last night. Today's client called just before five yesterday afternoon with a last-minute menu change. It seems one of her guests has a shellfish allergy, so the shrimp appetizer I'd planned was a no-go." She lifted her shoulders in a shrug.

"A caterer's work is never done."

"Exactly." She flashed a smile as they walked into the kitchen.

"Are you like this every weekend?" he asked.

"When I'm lucky."

Dan frowned at her reply. "Perhaps you should consider hiring more assistants. It sounds as if you could use the additional help."

She could. That was true enough. But adding more employees to the payroll was out of the question. Their wages and the additional taxes would eat too far into her profits. Emily figured she could work herself to near exhaustion on weekends for however long it took to open her restaurant. What else did she have going on Saturday nights anyway? When The Merit became a reality, she would gladly hire a full kitchen and wait-staff, and take off nights here and there when the mood struck. Until then, caffeine would be her best friend.

Which prompted her to ask, "Can I get you something to drink? Espresso? Coffee? Tea, maybe?"

"Coffee, since I see that you already have a pot prepared." He nodded in the direction of the state-of-the-art brewing station she'd splurged on the previous Christmas.

"Yeah. I switched to French roast after the espresso." She grinned. "I figured I'd better pace my caffeine intake. I can't afford to get jittery when I'm working with knives."

He smiled in return as he settled onto one of the tall stools at the granite-topped island. At the moment, the island was littered with a cornucopia of fresh produce that had already been washed. Some of it would be used in a salad. Others would be chopped and added to the various dishes.

As she poured them both a cup, he reminded her she hadn't answered his question about hiring more help. Emily didn't feel it would be professional to discuss finances with a paying client, so she edited her response before speaking.

"I've always loved cooking and creating new dishes, which is why I do what I do for a living. So, I don't mind the extra work." She handed him his coffee and sipped her own.

"But what do you do for pleasure?" he asked.

The exotic lilt in his voice caused the last word to feather over Emily's flesh like a caress, and it had her stammering like a schoolgirl.

"I…I…I…read." If he hadn't been watching her she would have smacked her forehead at the lame response. She didn't have to know Dan well to figure out he was sophisticated, educated and cultured. He probably could lead Met patrons on a guided tour of the museum's Egyptian antiquities exhibit. And she was certain he spent his free time engaged in far more *pleasurable* pursuits. Meanwhile, she sounded provincial and antisocial.

But he said, "I enjoy reading as well. Who are your favorite authors?"

Somehow she doubted rattling off a bunch of chef's names was going to improve her image. He already must think she was a workaholic.

"I don't really have any favorites," she hedged. "If a book looks like it might appeal to me, I pick it up."

"Very open-minded." He nodded.

"What about you? Do you have a favorite author?" He probably leaned toward the classics. He probably read Socrates' *Charmides* for fun.

"Stephen King."

"Stephen King?" She set her coffee cup down on the counter with a clunk.

"You seem surprised."

And he seemed amused. Emily wrinkled her nose and averred, "It's just that I wouldn't be able to sleep at night if I read his stuff."

"I sleep like a baby."

Dan's lips quirked up, drawing her attention to his mouth. He had a sexy mouth, very sensual, as her assistant had noted that evening at the Hendersons'. At that moment,

Emily could picture him sleeping, but not like a baby. He was all male and fully grown, lying between silk sheets and wearing... Emily cleared her throat. What was wrong with her?

"How on earth did we get on this subject?"

"We were talking about the long hours you work and what you do for pl—"

"Right!" She rudely cut him off, but she couldn't bear to hear that word slip from his gorgeous lips a second time, especially given the vastly inappropriate direction her thoughts had just strayed. "As I said, I really do love my job."

Work. Talk about work. Keep it about work, she coached herself, and decided it was time to get back to her cutting board.

"But with more employees you could take on more clients and still enjoy time for yourself. I am not familiar with your business. Do you cater large events?"

She shook her head. "No. I did a few large corporate parties when I was starting up. The money was welcome, but it felt a little too much like assembly-line work. I prefer small parties. I feel I have more control over the finished product that way."

"Ah." He dipped his head in understanding. "A perfectionist."

Emily chuckled. "My assistant would say I'm a control freak, but I like your word better."

"So this is your dream," he said, sounding almost wistful.

"For now."

"I am intrigued. What more do you want, Emily?"

The question was benign, but when a man looked like Dan Tarim, a woman kept imagining—or perhaps hoping—for subtext.

Motioning with her arms to encompass the kitchen, she said, "I have it all. What more could I want?"

"You tell me."

She almost wanted to, and not just about the restaurant, but the other hopes for her life, hopes she'd shoved to the back burner and rarely thought about these days: a husband. A family. A home.

Startled by the direction of her thoughts, she shook her head. "Another time, perhaps."

"Very well."

A bell chimed then and Emily crossed to the commercial-grade double oven. After donning protective mitts, she pulled out the dish inside and set it on a rack on the counter to cool.

The scent of cinnamon and apples wafting through the air was enough to make one's mouth water.

"That smells like heaven," Dan said. "What it is?"

"My favorite part of a meal: dessert."

"Is it apple pie?"

"Not quite. That seemed a little too American to serve with the French-inspired menu my client requested, so I opted for an apple-almond tart."

Dan walked over to inspect it, inhaling deeply as he went. "It looks too perfect to eat," he said. The apples were thinly sliced and perfectly arranged in a swirling pattern inside the thick crust.

"Wait till you see what I'm planning for you." When he turned she said, "A pear and caramel trifle heaped with whipped cream."

"That sounds like pure decadence." Dan's dark gaze turned intense and sensual enough to have her swallowing.

"P-perhaps *self-indulgence* would be a better word," she said.

Pleasure. Decadence. The man had an excellent grasp of the English vocabulary even though it was his second language.

"I prefer decadence." He smiled then and heat began to curl through her.

Though her hands were clean, Emily wiped them on the front of her apron. Her palms were damp. Overall, she felt uncomfortably warm. She blamed the oven and the rising temperature outside. Maybe she should turn up her air-conditioning. She glanced at Dan. He appeared perfectly comfortable and unperturbed.

It was time to get down to business, she decided.

"I think you'll approve of the rest of the meal I've planned."

With that, she went to her desk to retrieve the folder containing the menu for his dinner party.

Madani returned to his seat at the counter feeling a little off center. Thankfully he had long ago mastered the art of camouflaging his emotions. He wasn't sure how it had happened, but a simple conversation about dessert had turned into foreplay.

For him, at least.

In fact, ever since setting foot in her apartment-slash-place-of-business, he'd been acutely aware of Emily not as a chef but as a woman. He blamed his long hours this trip as well as the long absence of intimate female companionship for his libidinous thoughts.

Emily's appearance didn't help matters. She looked especially lovely today. Her hair was pulled back, no doubt out of deference for her work, but instead of a chignon, it was twisted in some fashion at the back that left it fuller in the front. The teal blouse was a good choice for her. It enhanced the color of her eyes and paired well with her creamy complexion. Without proper protection, her skin would burn in the hot sun of his homeland. He wondered if it was as soft as it appeared.

Dan sipped his coffee, which had grown cold. He, on the other hand, was becoming hot. Indeed, if they had spent another moment discussing decadent desserts, he might have wound up embarrassing himself.

As it was, he was pretty sure he'd embarrassed Emily. When she returned to the kitchen, he noticed that her cheeks were pink and she was careful to maintain her distance, even when she sat on the stool next to his, opened a folder and pushed it toward him on the counter. Should he apologize? He decided against it, partly because putting any of his veiled thoughts into words would surely only make matters more awkward.

Her expression was guarded, her voice crisply professional when she said, "We'll start with appetizers. You asked for two. Based on what you've told me about your guests and the kind of evening you have planned, I'm suggesting penne pasta with asparagus and basil. The portions will be larger than normal since you will be foregoing a salad course. In addition, and in a nod to your region of the world, I propose a hummus dish. It's made with chickpeas and lemon and uses yogurt instead of sesame paste. It will be accompanied by the customary wedges of toasted pita bread."

She glanced up, clearly expecting him to say something. So, he offered, "It sounds perfect."

"For the main course you wanted fish. I know you were a fan of the salmon I made for the Hendersons, so I'm hoping you'll be similarly pleased with the sea bass I plan to simmer in a light white wine sauce."

She leaned closer and pointed to the photograph she'd included in the folder. He thought he caught a hint of floral fragrance beneath the aromatic scents of the kitchen.

Emily was saying, "As you can see, I propose pairing it with risotto, which will be seasoned and formed into cakes that will be skillet fried. The textures mix well."

"Textures?"

"The fish is fork tender. The crispness of the risotto cakes offsets that."

"That makes sense," he said, surprised at how much thought she put into planning a meal.

"Finally, I will steam green beans over which I will shave the truffles you requested. I chose green beans, because I wanted to let the truffles shine without too many other competing flavors."

"The star of the show," he said.

"Exactly. What's the point otherwise?"

She glanced up and smiled. Talking about food had eased her earlier discomfort.

"Generally speaking, the meal is light, which is good considering what I've told you I will be making for dessert. Your guests will feel they are entitled to splurge."

"Very impressive. It appears you've thought of everything," he said.

"Well, that is what you're paying me for. Which reminds me." She flipped the page. "Since you're visiting the city, I took the liberty of quoting you prices for china place settings and silverware. I have service for thirty, including all of the matching serving pieces."

"Thank you, but that won't be necessary. The accommodations I keep in Manhattan have everything I need."

She nodded. "I've also listed a selection of wines, both white and red, that would pair well with the courses. I can pick them up for you and include them in my final price, or you can purchase them on your own if you prefer. If you do want to purchase them separately, I can suggest a location. The owner is a friend and he will give you a discount if you mention you're a client of mine."

Madani skimmed the list she'd provided. Again, he found himself impressed with the breadth of her knowledge. "You have a good eye for wine," he told her. Some of the vintages she'd included were quite pricey, but all of them were well-regarded.

"Wine is often an integral part of the meal. As such it can either enhance the flavors of what I've prepared or detract from them." She shrugged then and her expression turned rueful. "Control freak, remember?"

He shook his head. "Not a control freak. A perfectionist." Even though Madani knew it was foolhardy, he reached over and touched her face. He planned the contact to be brief, just a light brush of his fingertips over the slope of her skin. But his fingers lingered and his hand opened until his palm cupped the side of her face. "And a lovely perfectionist at that. *Gamila.*"

Before he even knew what he intended, he'd leaned in and kissed her opposite cheek. Even though he was stunned at what he had just done, he drew back slowly. What madness was this, he wondered, that had him wanting to kiss her again and on the lips this time?

Emily sat very still. Her eyes were wide, her gaze intent. "What does that mean?" she asked in a voice that was barely above a whisper.

"I do not know," he replied haltingly, truthfully. He wasn't sure what emotion he'd intended to express with his forward behavior.

"You don't know?" She appeared puzzled. "But you just said it."

"Said it? Ah." It dawned on him then that she was talking about the word he'd used, rather than seeking an explanation for his actions. "*Gamila* means beautiful in Arabic."

Her cheeks turned pink again. "Oh." She cleared her throat then, shifted back on her seat.

"You are beautiful, Emily."

She didn't look at him. "I'm a caterer."

"And you cannot be both?"

He saw her swallow. "About the wine, what do you want me to do?"

Irritation snapped within him. "I'll see to the wine."

"Okay."

He modified his tone. "I have a couple of the ones you've suggested on hand, as well as a favorite of mine that I plan to serve. I think it will meet with your approval."

She nodded and stood. "Well, that's that, then. Unless you want to change or add something to the menu."

"One cannot improve upon perfection," he replied, following her lead and rising to his feet.

Emily collected the folder and handed it to him. "The cost is broken down on the front. I require an advance payment of half the total amount, which is nonrefundable once I've purchased the ingredients. The remainder is due the night of the party."

"Will a personal check do?"

"Certainly."

He drew his checkbook from his pocket, wrote one out and handed it to her, wondering at the sudden awkwardness he felt. It seemed he should say something more, if only so he could linger awhile in her company and determine why he found her so fascinating. But a glance at his watch revealed that he'd taken up too much of her time already. How had an hour managed to pass so quickly?

"I should let you return to work," he said.

"Unfortunately I need to. I have a lot left to do." They walked to the door. As she opened it, she added, "I'll be in touch."

"Gee, Em, isn't that usually the guy's line on the morning after?" a man drawled insultingly from the hallway, where he stood on the welcome mat with his hand raised as if to knock. He was fair-haired and nearly the same height as Madani. "And here poor Elle is worried that the reason you won't stand up in the wedding is you haven't gotten over me."

The man's gaze was as insolent as it was measuring when it shifted to Madani.

"Take care with your words," Madani said. He kept his voice soft, but the threat was unmistakable.

"Who is this guy, Em?"

"What are you doing here, Reed? What do you want?"

The man ignored her questions. Instead, he persisted, "Aren't you going to introduce me to your boyfriend? Maybe I can offer him some insights into your...likes and dislikes."

Madani took a step forward at the same time Emily laid a hand on his arm. "I'm sorry, Dan. This rude and obnoxious man is Reed Benedict, my sister's fiancé."

Sister's fiancé? Yet Reed's previous words implied he and Emily had been a couple.

"I see you're trying to connect the dots." The man named Reed winked as he stretched out a hand. "I wanted to keep it in the family."

Emily had called him rude and obnoxious. Madani silently added a few more adjectives to the list, and while he wasn't the sort of man prone to violence, he found himself wanting to take a swing at Reed's arrogant face. To keep from acting on the impulse, he curled his hand into a fist, which he kept at his side.

"I don't believe Emily wants you here. Maybe you should leave."

Reed lowered the hand Madani had refused to shake. "Word to the wise. Em doesn't like guys to speak for her. She's too *independent* for that."

The man's tone turned the trait into a character flaw. Incensed on her behalf, Madani asked Emily, "Shall I make him leave?"

She blinked in surprise. "As tempting as I find your offer, no. I'll give him five minutes of my time. You can go now. I'll call you later in the week."

Left with no choice, Madani bid her goodbye.

CHAPTER FOUR

ONCE THEY WERE ALONE, Emily let the full range of her wrath sharpen her tone. "What are you doing here, Reed?"

"Elle asked me to come." He sloughed off his sports coat as if she'd asked him to make himself more comfortable and flung it over one thick arm of the love seat. His voice held a sneer when he said, "I see that you've done a lot to the place since I've been gone."

The jerk smiled then, flashing several thousand dollars worth of veneers. She'd paid the bills for a couple of months so that he could afford them.

"I made it more suited to my needs," she agreed.

"Your needs. That's funny." His smile turned nasty. "I didn't think you had any."

The blow hit below the belt, just as he'd intended. Reed had always been good at stripping away her femininity, turning her into some sort of asexual automaton simply because she had dreams that went beyond being a showpiece on his arm.

It struck Emily then that she didn't feel that way around Dan. Okay, she didn't know the man well—hardly at all, come to that—but she had never been more aware of her femininity, her sexuality than when he was around.

She folded her arms, her confidence returning. "I'm busy today, so you'll have to get to the point of your visit."

"Busy. Always busy." He sighed. "Too busy, apparently, to make time for your family."

"Don't try to send me on a guilt trip, Reed. I have absolutely no guilt where you and Elle are concerned." She raised her chin a notch, a gesture she knew he found irritating. Sure enough, he scowled.

"She wants you at the shower tomorrow afternoon, Em. God only knows why since you're so bitter and jealous. You'll probably ruin the day for her."

Emily's brow rose. "Is this your idea of appealing to my better nature?" she asked, almost as amused as she was irritated.

"No. You don't have one of those," he shot back. "I never realized you could be so vindictive."

"Bitter, jealous *and* vindictive. Wow. That's some trifecta."

"I'm serious. Elle and I feel sorry for you. You spend every waking hour wrapped up in your work." He motioned toward the kitchen and shook his head. He'd never understood her, she realized now, wondering how she'd put up with his belittling comments. That much hadn't changed. "The kitchen in this place is now three times the size of the bedroom. Not that you probably care."

"I don't."

He shook his head. You're going to wind up sad and alone."

Even as she raised her chin, Emily swallowed, hating that he'd found yet another chink in her armor. "Don't waste your time pitying me, Reed. I'm really quite happy."

Happy and alone, a little voice whispered. *Happy with a thriving career*, she silently shot back. God, she was not only arguing with her ex, but she was arguing with her subconscious.

"Right." He shook his head. "You keep telling yourself that, Em."

She dropped her arms to her sides in exasperation and started for the door. "I'd say that your job here is done. You've delivered Elle's message."

"And?"

"Tell her I don't think I can make it, but if I manage to wrap things up early tomorrow, I'll stop in."

"That's big of you." His tone suggested he felt otherwise.

"Goodbye, Reed." Emily opened the apartment door and allowed a little of her own pettiness to seep through. "I'd say it was good seeing you, but it wasn't."

One step from leaving, he stopped. For an uncomfortable moment he stared at her. "It's hard to believe that we were ever a couple, let alone for so long. I don't know who you are anymore, Emily."

She could have said the same. Instead, she told him, "I haven't changed. I always had these dreams, these goals. They're why I went to culinary school in the first place."

"Yeah, but I didn't think they'd pan out for you, at least not to the extent that they have."

"You thought I'd fail?" He wasn't the only one left wondering how they'd ever become a couple.

"Not fail exactly. I just figured that you would make a nice little hobby of it, you know?"

No. She didn't know. "A nice little hobby?" His lack of faith shouldn't have come as a surprise, let alone as a blow. Oddly, it hurt almost as much as his romantic defection had. "Well, Elle's goals shouldn't be a problem for you."

Reed's brow furrowed. "She doesn't have any goals."

"Exactly."

Emily closed the door behind him. She slammed it, actually. And even though she tried to banish their conversation from her mind, his prediction that she would wind up sad and alone pecked at her peace for the rest of the day.

* * *

Madani's eyes were closed as he reclined on the chaise on his terrace. The afternoon sun felt good on his face, as did the breeze that accompanied it. Music floated from the stereo, a languid melody with lyrics to match. He should have been relaxed. Indeed, he gave the appearance of being so. But he was far from it.

He'd returned from Emily's apartment several hours ago far too keyed up to work. He'd paced, put himself through a punishing workout with the free weights he kept in one of the spare rooms. Neither had helped.

Even sitting on the terrace doing nothing was proving difficult. He wanted to break something.

He had a feeling he would have felt this way even if he hadn't also had the misfortune of meeting her ex-boyfriend just before taking his leave.

Madani wasn't prone to snap judgments, but he'd made an exception in Reed Benedict's case. He didn't like him. The man had hurt Emily. That much was clear. He was marrying her sister. But it was the rude way in which the man had spoken to her that bothered Madani the most. His verbal jabs were proof that he disrespected her.

"I should have punched him," he muttered aloud.

"I hope you are not talking about me, *sadiqi*. Though only for your sake."

Madani opened his eyes as a chuckling Azeem stepped out onto the terrace.

"Not this time." Swinging his legs to the flagstone floor he rose. "Care to join me for a drink?"

"What kind of drink?"

"The only kind that counts when a man is in a foul mood."

Azeem's bushy eyebrows shot up at that. "An alcoholic beverage this early in the day? Something serious must be troubling you. Or could it be someone?"

The question hit a little too close for comfort. "Do you want a drink or not?" Madani snapped impatiently.

"Of course. I would never pass up an opportunity to sample your cognac. I cannot afford such superior quality on the salary you pay me."

"Maybe I should sack you and be done with it."

His friend merely smiled. "If you'd like we can discuss the terms of my termination over the cognac."

When Madani returned with their drinks, Azeem had pulled a padded wrought-iron chair over from the table. "So, whom do you wish to strike?"

Picturing Benedict's overconfident sneer, Madani's blood boiled anew. "This...this fool of a man who... Forget it. He is not worth another moment of my time."

He would leave it at that, Madani decided. He handed Azeem one of the snifters and settled back on his chaise.

Azeem sipped his cognac. Nodding sagely, he said, "A woman is involved."

"Why must there be a woman involved?" Madani asked in exasperation.

"Because all too often men are fools where women are concerned." Despite Azeem's smile, his expression lacked its usual joviality.

"The voice of experience, my friend?"

Azeem merely shrugged. "Aren't we all fools at one time or another when it comes to women? Well, except for you, of course. Even as you prepare to marry one of Kashaqra's loveliest specimens, you will never be a fool for a woman. You do not believe in love."

Madani's eyes narrowed. "I have the feeling you have just insulted me."

"Never. I am but your humble servant." Azeem's lips twitched below his dark mustache.

"Now I know I have been insulted."

"So who is this woman?"

Madani swirled the cognac in his snifter. The color of the liquid reminded him of Emily's hair. "No one you know. I have just met her myself."

"Yet she weighs on your mind and inspires you to violence." Azeem's lips turned down in consideration. "That's quite an accomplishment."

Madani didn't care for his friend's summation since it was too close to the truth. He planned to change the subject, but the words that slipped out were, "She is so much more than what some people see."

"Including the fool?"

"Especially the fool." He snorted, drained his glass. "He had her and he didn't appreciate her."

Azeem hoisted his snifter, emptied it. "I know exactly what you mean."

The following morning, Emily knew to expect at least one phone call from her mother, if not half a dozen. Elle's shower was at two o'clock, which meant Miranda would be in overdrive.

Sure enough, the telephone in Emily's apartment rang just after she returned from a brutal workout at the gym. After a peek at the Caller ID, Emily was tempted not to answer, but Miranda would try her cell and then alternate between the two for the next couple of hours until Emily finally picked up. Better to get this over with now so that she could attempt to enjoy the rest of her day.

Grabbing the cordless receiver, she flopped down on the couch. "Hi, Mom."

"Oh, I'm so relieved to hear your voice. Are you all right, honey?"

Hmm. This was a new tactic. "Why wouldn't I be?" she asked.

"Well, Reed and Elle are here, and Reed mentioned that a strange man was at your apartment yesterday."

Ah. Mystery solved. "The only strange man at my apartment yesterday was Reed. The other one was a client of mine."

"A client. Oh." Miranda sounded disappointed.

"Are you sorry it wasn't a serial murderer?"

"Don't be silly," her mother chided. "It's just, I guess I was hoping…well, you know."

"Hoping what?" Emily asked, perfectly aware she would regret doing so.

"That maybe you'd found someone."

She expelled an exasperated sigh. "Mom, you need to make up your mind. A moment ago you claimed to be worried that the man Reed met yesterday might have harmed me and now you're disappointed that I'm not involved with the guy."

"Oh, please," Miranda huffed. "Forgive me for being a little excited that you might have found someone. Reed mentioned that the man was there early in the morning."

"It was nearly eleven o'clock, Mother." Emily snorted. "That's only early for Reed.

I'd been up working for hours. And this was business. As I said, Dan is a client."

"Dan, hmm?"

"Yes. Dan. Generally speaking, I'm on a first-name basis with all of my clients."

"Client or not, Reed said the man was possessive of you. He said he was a little surprised that you allowed it."

Emily thought back on the exchange. Possessive? No, she wouldn't have allowed that. Protective was more like it. And that she didn't mind. Indeed, she smiled now, recalling the way Dan had told Reed to watch his words and later had offered to toss him out. Despite all of his refinement and sophistication, she had little doubt he would have done so—and quite handily—had she agreed. It almost made her wish she'd let him.

Forcing herself back to the present, Emily said, "Is this the only reason you're calling, Mom?"

"No," Miranda replied.

"I didn't think so," Emily mumbled. Heaven knew she couldn't get that lucky.

"Reed told me why he stopped to see you yesterday. He also told me the cool reception his request received." Miranda's voice lowered. "I'm really disappointed in you, Emily Josephine."

Emily massaged her forehead. She was pushing thirty and her mother was still trotting out her middle name in the hope of forcing her to toe the line. "For what, Mom? Not dropping everything to be at Elle's side today?"

She said it sarcastically, but her mother took her words at face value. "Yes."

"I've got work to do." Which wasn't a complete fabrication. She could always find something business-related to occupy her time.

But her mother called her on it. "That's a convenient excuse and we both know it. Just stop in for five minutes today, not just for Elle's sake but to put the rumors to rest."

That got her attention. "Rumors?"

"You know your aunt Dora. Your cousin Sara says she's claiming you're too broken up over losing Reed to put in an appearance."

"Hardly."

"I know," Miranda agreed with an airy sigh. "I told Sara to tell her as much, but Aunt Dora's already been on the phone to

Aunt Betty and Aunt Sally. She told them that you're all but incapacitated with heartache and that's why it's unlikely you will be at the shower today."

Emily's molars ground together. She knew she was being manipulated. She knew it! Yet on the off chance her mother was telling the truth and the aunts were burning up the grapevine with tales of her woe, pride demanded that she put in an appearance.

Brokenhearted, indeed.

It struck Emily then that she wasn't. At least not as much as she should have been given the fact that she'd thought she and Reed would wed eventually. God, they'd dated for so long. She was ticked off, sure. As she saw it, she had every right to be. But the fact was, given the same set of opportunities, Emily would make the same choices all over again.

"What time will you finish playing Bridal Bingo and all of the other silly games?" she asked.

Miranda's tone was triumphant, confirming Emily's worst fears. "Oh, we'll be done with those no later than three."

"I can only stay an hour."

"Terrific." She pictured her mother rubbing her hands together in glee. Miranda—and Elle—had gotten their way. Again. "See you this afternoon, dear. Oh, and since your sister's bridesmaid dresses will be peach, we thought it would be nice for members of the wedding party to wear something in that color."

CHAPTER FIVE

EMILY CHOSE RED.

The dress' low cut was inappropriate for a Sunday afternoon not to mention a bridal shower. She didn't care. She paired it with lethal pumps and a kiss-off attitude. If she was riddled with remorse over her breakup with Reed and his subsequent engagement to her baby sister, it looked damned good on her, she decided, adding a bit more kohl liner to her eyes.

She finished off the dramatic look with lipstick in the same flaming shade as her dress. Yes, she was being defiant, but she wouldn't give in entirely to her mother's manipulations.

Miranda's mouth pinched tight when Emily walked through the door of her family's two-story Brooklyn home. The guests, which included all of the aunts and female cousins, as well as a gaggle of Elle's girlfriends, were gathered in the living room. Her mother jumped up from her place next to Elle and crossed to Emily.

"That's not peach," she hissed as she pretended to kiss her daughter's cheek.

"Nope. It's not even close."

Elle came up next, looking like a confection in her white eyelet sundress with its wide peach sash. Blond hair tumbled around a face whose pouty, glossed lips would have been right at home on the cover of a men's magazine.

Emily had once overheard their father say where Elle would stop traffic, Emily would be the one to give out the tickets. Darin Merit hadn't meant it as a compliment. She'd decided to take it as one anyway.

"Oh, Em!" Elle exclaimed, enveloping Emily in a hug that was tight enough to transfer the overpowering scent of her perfume to Emily's skin. "You've made my day! Your being here is truly the best gift of all."

This was said loudly enough for those at the far end of the room to hear without straining. The murmuring began almost immediately. Emily couldn't make out what the guests were saying, but their gazes were full of pity and speculation, making the words unnecessary.

"I brought you something anyway." She pulled out of the death grip long enough to fetch the gift she'd set on the console table in the foyer.

"Here."

"I'm sure I'll love it," Elle said, clasping the wrapped box to her bosom.

Emily doubted it. She hadn't had time to shop off Elle's gift registry and the sisters had never shared the same taste, Reed being the exception. "I've included the receipt just in case."

"Why don't you help yourself to some refreshment, Emily, and then join us," her mother suggested.

Emily glanced at the clock. It was five minutes past three. The games were done. She only had to endure this charade for another fifty-five minutes. Less than the amount of time it took for her to whip up a soufflé. Some punch would help, she decided.

Especially if her aunt Sally had already managed to spike it with rum.

In the kitchen, she ladled up a glass of punch as red as her dress. A sip had her closing her eyes. "Bless you, Aunt Sally," she murmured and returned to the living room.

Unfortunately a glance around confirmed her worst fears. The only seat available was next to Aunt Dora.

"You look ready for a night on the town," Aunt Dora remarked.

"I'm going out later." The lie slipped easily from Emily's lips. "I won't have enough time to get back to my apartment afterward, so..." She sipped more punch.

"Oh?" Her aunt's face lit up. "Do you have a new man in your life?"

Her thoughts turned to Dan. "It's not serious or anything. We've just met."

"Is he handsome?" Her aunt's elbow dug into her ribs.

"God, yes. Drop-dead gorgeous is more like it." That wasn't a lie.

Dora reached over and squeezed her hand. "I'm so happy that you're moving on."

A mouthful of punch went down smoothly. "Oh, yeah. The ship has sailed," Emily confirmed.

She hoped that would be the end of it, but of course it wasn't. Dora found a new reason to pity her.

"It must be hard, though, to watch your baby sister get married first. Goodness, she's nearly six years younger than you are! But at least you're seeing someone now."

Emily made a noncommittal sound. Not that it mattered. Dora went on.

"And you still have time. You don't turn thirty for—what?—another year yet." Eight and a half months. Emily hadn't been counting. Until now.

Dora went on. "My Christine says a lot of women feel the need to have a career before settling down, just so they know what they're *not* missing once they do."

Ah, yes, Christine. The voice of experience. She was the same age as Elle and had tied the knot in a hastily ordered civil ceremony a month out of high school. Aunt Dora still claimed little Jimmy had been born premature, though no one in the family believed that at eight pounds, seven ounces he'd arrived two months early.

"It's a rat race out there," Emily agreed, managing to sound sincere. Another gulp of punch helped.

"All those long hours you put in and for what? So you can go home all alone?" Aunt Dora shook her head in dismay and reached over for Emily's free hand. "Thank God you've met someone. Maybe now Elle won't get too much of a head start on you."

"That would be tragic." Her glass was empty, which was just as well. She was already feeling a bit tipsy.

A moment later, though, when her mother announced they would be playing a game to determine which guest knew Elle and Reed the best, Emily decided on a refill.

Madani had no reason to call Emily. The menu for the following Saturday was set, the down payment had been made. But as he prowled restlessly around his rooms at The Mark on Sunday afternoon, he tried to come up with one. As happened whenever he set his mind to something, he succeeded.

Flipping open his cell phone, he punched in the business number from Emily's card. When her recorded voice greeted him, he cursed and hung up without leaving a message. Not one to give up, though, he eyed the card again. Her cell number was on it, too.

When she answered he could barely make out her voice over the din of conversation in the background. He assumed she was working, probably whipping up her magic in some wealthy socialite's kitchen.

"Dan. This is a surprise."

"It sounds as if I'm interrupting something," he said apologetically. "I'll hang up and let you get back to whatever it is you're doing."

"No!" Even with the background noise, her shout came across as desperate.

"Emily, is everything all right?"

"Not even close." Her tone was wry. "I'm glad you called, actually."

The pleasure he experienced upon hearing her say that was way out of proportion. Even so, he couldn't stop it.

"I...I need a favor," she said.

"Anything." He meant it.

"Have you ever been to Brooklyn?"

Azeem didn't say a word during the drive. He didn't have to. His smirk said it all, which was why Madani felt the need to explain, to put things into proper perspective. For his friend. For himself.

As they crossed from lower Manhattan to Brooklyn, Madani said, "It's not what you are thinking."

"What am I thinking?"

"That I have taken your advice. That I am having this, this *fling* you suggested."

"Aren't you?"

"No!" The protest only made him sound guilty.

"I make no judgments, Madani. I, better than anyone, know that the arrangement you have with Nawar doesn't make it a love match."

"No, but I am not having a fling."

Azeem shrugged with maddening indifference.

"Emily asked me to collect her." Indeed, her voice had verged on pleading. She'd promised to explain the situation to him in full later. "I am doing a favor for a friend. Nothing more."

"So, now she is a friend rather than a caterer." The smirk was back.

"She can be both, can she not? You are my driver as well as my friend," he pointed out.

"True." Azeem didn't sound convinced, though. "And perhaps you are a fool."

Azeem muttered it half under his breath, leaving Madani to wonder if he had heard correctly.

"What?"

"Nothing."

Madani stared out his window. A yellow taxi blasted past. Couldn't Azeem go any faster? A moment later, he ran a hand over his face. He should have shaved. Though a little scruff on a man's cheeks was in fashion these days, he preferred a smooth face when he went out with a woman. But this wasn't a date, he reminded himself. Nor was it business. It was…a rescue of sorts.

Twenty minutes later, Azeem pulled the car to a stop in front a comfortable-looking two-story house on an oak-lined street in Brooklyn.

"Are you sure this is the right address?" Azeem's tone was dubious.

"It's what she said."

He opened the car door and stepped out, feeling oddly apprehensive as he navigated the flower-lined stoop, and that was before he spied the pair of white paper wedding bells hanging over the door. Under the bells were the names "Reed and Elle."

What was he getting himself into? No doubt a family drama every bit as melodramatic as his own tended to be.

He knocked anyway. A moment later an ample-chested matron opened the door. She eyed him frankly before breaking into laughter, and called over her shoulder, "Miranda, you didn't mention there would be male entertainment at this shower."

"Good Lord, Sally! Get away from the door."

Another woman appeared then. This one wasn't smiling. "Can I help you?"

"I've come for Emily."

"Emily?" She frowned.

"Emily Merit. Is she here?" he inquired politely.

"Yes." The woman pushed open the screen door and invited him inside, albeit reluctantly.

Stepping into the living room, Madani knew a moment of panic. It was filled with women, a good three dozen of them, and they were sizing him up like a prized camel.

He fell back on manners. "Good afternoon, ladies."

His gaze landed on Emily then. She was tucked between two large matrons. Where all of the other women were adorned in pastels, she wore red. Vivid, vibrant, sexy red. She uncrossed a pair of surprisingly long legs and rose to her feet. The dress flaunted her curves.

"Ah, my knight in shining armor has arrived." Her lips quirked with a smile that would have been right at home on a siren. The blood in his head started heading south. And this was before she said, "I'm sorry to have to leave the party early, but I have other plans for the rest of the afternoon and maybe the evening."

She sent a wink in the direction of the woman who had first opened the door.

"Em, aren't you going to introduce us to your…your friend?" a young woman asked.

Based on the corsage, he assumed her to be the guest of honor, making her Emily's sister. The two women didn't look much alike.

"Oh, yes. How rude of me. This is Dan. I'm catering a party for him, which makes him a client. Our relationship is *strictly* business." The way she said it implied otherwise.

"So, you're just going to leave?" the blonde asked petulantly. She was curvy and attractive, but not his type at all.

"Yep. Sorry. I am. But you know me, Elle. All work and no play. Dull, dull, dull." Emily's laughter was throaty and shot straight to his loins.

Swallowing, Madani watched her weave toward him through the crowded living room, stepping around guests, wrapped boxes and gift bags. Her gaze was smoldering and direct, if a little unfocused. When she reached him, she framed his face with her hands, rose up on tiptoe and kissed him full on the mouth.

That was all it took. Though he had no right, not to mention an audience, he kissed her back. How could he not?

Mmm.

The sound was like a gunshot in the quiet room. Had he moaned or had she? Either way, the satisfied vocalization was fitting. This was good. Better than he'd fantasized, he thought, admitting to himself that he had indeed fantasized.

"Oh, for heaven's sake!" someone shouted. Her mother, most likely.

Madani ended the kiss, but only because Emily had begun to pull away. She appeared undaunted despite the whispers going on around them. In fact, she grinned, that impish dimple serving only to stoke his appetite.

"What do you say we get out of here?"

CHAPTER SIX

HIS REACTION NOTWITHSTANDING, Madani knew all was not as it seemed. Something more was going on. Emily confirmed as much the moment they were outside.

As he escorted her down the steps to his car, she drew to a halt. "I'm sorry about that."

"The kiss?" Even though he'd expected it, her apology served as a bucket of ice water. "I didn't mind."

She glanced sideways at him and her cheeks turned pink. "I meant it when I said you were my knight in shining armor. I planned to leave my sister's bridal shower early, but there seemed to be no way to exit gracefully without having to endure their pity, especially since I left my vehicle in the city and would have to call a car."

"Why would they pity you?"

Her tone turned wry. "Well, let's see, it probably has something to do with the fact that my baby sister is not only getting married first, she's marrying the man I dated for six years."

"Their betrayal must have hurt you deeply." He said it softly, reaching up to tuck a stray curl behind her ear.

She stilled, studied him. "You know, you're one of the few people who get that. My parents seem to think I should be delighted beyond measure that Elle is finally settling down, even if she's doing it with my ex, who *wasn't* my ex when she began seeing him."

Madani had wanted to take a swing at Benedict when they'd met the day before and that was without knowing what a duplicitous cretin he was.

"Elle, of course, blathers on about how she *always* had a crush on Reed and that *nothing* can stand in the way of true love."

"And Reed?"

Emily huffed out a breath. "He claims to be justified in cheating with my sister since my career can be so demanding."

"It sounds as if he felt threatened by you."

"Would you be?"

"Excuse me?"

She shook her head. "Never mind. Just a hypothetical question that I had no business asking." She sucked in a deep breath and let it out slowly. Though he thought she might say something more, she remained silent.

"I'll take you home."

At his signal, Azeem got out of the car parked at the curb and opened the rear door.

Emily grimaced. "Oh God. I didn't realize you had a driver. I've put both of you out, and on a Sunday afternoon no less."

"Not at all. Azeem had nothing better to do." In a stage whisper, he added, "He really needs a social life. It's sad really. I worry about him."

She laughed, as he'd intended, and Azeem joined in.

"I'd have a social life if not for Madani. I'm always at his beck and call."

"Madani?" Emily glanced back at him.

"It's my given name."

She smiled, nodded. "It suits you. I like it much better than Dan. Would you mind if I called you Madani from now on?"

She could call him whatever she wanted. He merely nodded, though, and helped her into the backseat. Ignoring Azeem's raised eyebrows, Madani followed suit. As the Mercedes started back to Manhattan, Emily leaned her head back against the rest, closed her eyes and sighed.

"Bad day?" he asked softly.

"Yes. Thanks again for doing this. It's only a slight exaggeration to say I thought I was going to die in there." She turned her head toward him and opened her eyes. "Or go insane. My mother has that effect. Add in a couple dozen aunts and female cousins and…"

Since his mother and some of the other women of his family could produce the same reaction in him, he commiserated. "I think I know what you mean."

"The punch didn't help."

"The punch?" Had someone harmed her?

"One of my aunts spiked it with rum and, given the way my head feels right now, I'm guessing she didn't hold back." Her gaze lost its focus as she admitted, "I had three glasses."

"Ah. Punch." Not sure what else to say, he nodded.

"I wouldn't have had so much if not for the game. You wouldn't know this, being a man and from a foreign country and all, but women here play the most ridiculous games at bridal showers."

Out of the corner of his eye, Madani caught a glimpse of Azeem in the rearview mirror. His friend's eyes were watering from suppressed laughter. No doubt, Madani would be hearing about this later.

"I'll take your word for it. So what was this game?"

"Twenty questions to determine which shower guest knew the bride-to-be and her intended groom the best."

Madani winced on Emily's behalf.

"Yeah, exactly. What quality does Reed admire most about Elle?" she intoned breezily. "Who said I love you first? Where did they go on their first date?"

"The first date they had behind your back."

"Yep." She closed her eyes, nodded. "That would be the one."

No wonder she'd drank so much of the punch. No wonder she'd kissed him.

"I'm sorry, Emily."

"Thanks." She snorted then. "A couple of my aunts actually seemed surprised that I didn't win."

Hoping to lighten the mood, he asked, "What was the prize if you had?"

Her nose wrinkled. "A set of hand towels embroidered with Elle's and Reed's names and their wedding date."

"Perhaps it's for the best that you lost. That doesn't sound like much of a prize."

Her tone was wry. "You don't think so? Elle did, but then she believes the whole world revolves around her."

"From what little I know of her intended, he believes the world revolves around him. It would seem, then, that they deserve one another."

She grinned sideways at him. "You, Madani Tarim, are definitely a bright spot in what has otherwise been a dark day."

"I'm glad I could be of service." He tried to ignore the fact Azeem's shoulders were now shaking with mirth.

They drove in silence for the next few minutes. Madani's conscience, however, was not quiet. Take Emily directly home, it commanded. He ignored it, and instead asked, "Are you hungry?"

"I am. Starving, in fact. My mother made the food," she explained. "Everything was overcooked and overspiced."

"Obviously you didn't get your talent in the kitchen from her."

"No. My mother's family came from the South originally. Three generations removed, deep-frying everything from meat to vegetables remains sacrosanct. When I started cooking as a teenager, it was a matter of self-preservation." She smiled. His breath caught. "Then it clicked and I knew I'd found my calling."

At that moment, Madani felt a calling as well, an irresistible urge to be with her in the only way he could. "Have dinner with me, Emily."

"I'd love to."

Emily meant it, which was why she suddenly felt so nervous. Foggy as her brain still felt, she knew this wasn't a good idea. But sitting beside Madani, steeped in his warmth and the subtle scent of his cologne as the

Mercedes sped through traffic, the exact reasons escaped her.

"Where shall we go?" he asked. "Do you have any preferences?"

Preferences? Indeed, yes, as a chef she had them. She was always eager to try new places or revisit those whose fare inspired her to make new creations. But at the moment her mind was dangerously blank. She couldn't think of the name of a single eatery either within the limits of Manhattan or the surrounding boroughs.

"Surprise me," she said. As if she really needed any more of those today.

Madani nodded and leaned forward to say something to the driver in their native tongue. Though Emily had no idea the content of his words, she liked their lyrical cadence.

"Will Azeem be joining us?" she asked politely as Madani settled back in his seat. She hoped the driver would. Surely having a chaperone along would ensure that things remained platonic, innocent.

Azeem grinned at her around his headrest. "Thank you for the invitation, but I believe there's a saying in your language about three being a crowd."

Emily managed a weak laugh. The kiss she'd planted on Madani in her parents' living room mocked her now. Nothing about it had been platonic or innocent. That had been her intent at the time, of course. She'd wanted to eradicate every last bit of pity oozing out of her aunts and cousins.

Poor Emily.

How many times had she heard that whispered during that hideous game? In some cases, a sympathetic glance in her direction had accompanied the words making it all but impossible to pretend she hadn't heard them.

And, okay, Em could admit that she'd used that kiss to prove to her mother and sister that she wasn't some spinster workaholic whose life lacked any trace of excitement or passion.

What she hadn't expected when she'd crossed the room and reached her intended target was for Madani to rest his hands on her waist, to draw her into his arms until they were pressed together from chest to thigh and then kiss her back.

And, oh, how the man could kiss. That much was obvious straight away, the brevity of the encounter notwithstanding.

The mere memory of it now sent heat curling through her. Even so, she shivered.

"Are you cold?" he asked.

Before she could respond, he'd ordered Azeem to turn down the air-conditioning and had peeled off his coat, which he then put around her shoulders.

Cold? No. Quite the opposite and now that she was all but cocooned in his scent her temperature threatened to shoot up by several more degrees. But she smiled, accepted his kindness and tried not to inhale too deeply lest she make a bigger fool of herself.

Emily was so preoccupied making nervous small talk for the next twenty minutes that she paid no attention to where they were heading until the car stopped. They were in Chinatown, she realized. They stepped out onto one of the narrow, winding streets just off Mott and not far from the heart of the ethnic neighborhood.

She gave no thought to masking either her surprise or her disappointment.

"Chinese food? But I thought…" Manners

finally caught up with her and she let the comment go unfinished.

Madani read her mind. "You were under the impression I would take you to a place that serves the types of food found in my country."

"Well, yes," she admitted.

In truth, she had looked forward to it. Perhaps because of her profession, Emily had an adventurous palate. She enjoyed trying new kinds of cuisine, loved identifying the spices and reveling in the textures. She couldn't say she'd ever eaten Kashaqra's fare, but in general she loved Middle Eastern food. Over the years, she'd added her own twists to standards such as tabouli and fattoush, and incorporated them into clients' menus, always to rave reviews.

The scents that greeted her as she stood outside Fuwang's were not cumin and turmeric, but sesame and ginger. Madani took her arm as they strolled toward the main entrance. Paper lanterns and banners written in Chinese characters dangled overhead.

"I would, but I have found only one or two places that I believe reflect the true taste of Kashaqra's cuisine."

"Are they close to here?" she asked hopefully.

"Not far. But neither has what you would call ambiance."

"What, no tablecloths or candles?" she teased. "I'm really not that high maintenance. I'd rather a quality meal than a fancy dining room."

"These lack that as well. Takeout only."

"Oh."

"I decided you would think it presumptuous of me to bring you back to my suite to dine." His dark gaze dipped, lingered on her mouth. Food was forgotten, pushed back behind thoughts of that kiss.

"Actually it would be quicker to go to my apartment than trek all the way to The Mark on the Upper East Side." She was staring at his mouth now, too. Nice lips, soft and firm at the same time. Just as his hold had been. "If you wait too long things might get cold."

Emily coughed. God, had she really just said that? Talk about sounding presumptuous. In the hope of resurrecting her self-respect, she added, "The food, I mean."

His lips twitched with a smile, telling her

that the extra words had only made it more obvious that her thoughts had strayed far from takeout meals.

Once again, Emily attempted to dig herself out of her self-dug hole. "But that's neither here nor there. We're in Chinatown."

Madani frowned now. "You do like Chinese food, don't you?"

She laughed, finally at ease now that the topic was something truly safe. "I just plain like food, Madani."

"Good, because I have a weakness for fried rice."

"Shrimp or chicken?"

He grinned, flashing straight white teeth. "Either, especially at Fuwang's."

Emily knew what he meant when their meals arrived half an hour later as they sat in the restaurant's sparsely populated dining room. Outside, the late June afternoon was winding down over a crowd on the sidewalk, but it would be a couple of hours yet before the dinner rush arrived.

Madani had ordered an appetizer of shrimp toasts, which they'd already polished off. Now, their waitress, a petite young woman dwarfed by the huge platter of food she carried, arrived with the rest of their meal.

There was so much of it.

Emily had gone for a traditional sweet and sour pork dish served with white rice. It wasn't exactly low-calorie with its sugary sauce and batter-dipped meat, but Emily figured she had endured the kind of day that begged for comfort food, and this fit the bill.

But she barely spared her plate a second glance after the waitress left. Madani had ordered hot sesame beef, but it was the side of shrimp-fried rice that held her attention. Peeking from the browned rice were a good dozen shrimp. Not salad-size either, but big enough to be classified as jumbo.

"I'm beginning to think I ordered the wrong thing," she commented.

"Would you like some?"

Though her mouth actually watered, she shook her head and said lightly, "We don't know one another well enough for me to eat off of your plate."

"That would be the second date?"

Uh-oh. The D word. Is that what he

thought this was? What she had led him to believe? She nearly groaned. If he did, she had no one to blame but herself after that wholly inappropriate lip-lock. Sure, she'd explained it away afterward, but there was a reason for the saying: actions speak louder than words.

Over the quiet conversations of the other diners, Emily could hear music, airy flutes accompanied by the almost mournful sound of string instruments. It fit her current mood perfectly.

"Madani," she began.

He held up a hand, stopping her. "You are going to tell me we are not on a date. Am I right?" His gaze was as direct as his words.

"I think I may have given you the wrong impression earlier." She straightened in her seat, coughed. "Back at my parents' house."

"When you kissed me, you mean?"

Emily figured she had turned the same shade as the prancing dragon that adorned the festive wall mural. "Yes. Then."

"Will it offend you if I say I enjoyed it?" One dark brow shot up.

"I…I…" She might have continued stammering if he had not spared her by going on.

"You did not give me the wrong impression, Emily. Afterward, you made your reasons for kissing me very, very clear."

"Oh. Well…good." She shifted back in her seat, wishing those reasons were as clear to her right now as she studied his handsome face and considered leaning across the table to kiss him again. "I just wanted…" Uh-oh, don't go there. Starting over, she said, "It's just that we have a business relationship."

He smiled warmly. A little too warmly. "Yes."

"I think it would be best for it to stay that way." She said it and told herself that she meant it even as something she refused to admit might be disappointment did a little shimmy-shake through her stomach.

Emily thought she saw something dim in his dark eyes, but his expression and demeanor remained unchanged. Indeed, his voice sounded matter-of-fact when he replied, "We are in perfect agreement."

They ate in silence for a moment. Then Madani plucked one of the plump shrimp from the browned rice with his chopsticks and dropped it onto the side of her plate.

A peace offering? Apparently so.

"Maybe, in addition to having a business relationship, we also can be friends?"

"Friends?" The word sounded foreign to her ears.

"Yes."

She blinked, smiled. "I'd like that. Truly I would. Friends."

As they finished their meal, Emily knew she should have felt relieved. It was for the best. After all, what else beyond friendship could come from this…this relationship? Madani would be leaving the country soon, returning to his homeland in the Middle East. She had dreams of her own to pursue after his departure, plans that would require every last bit of her energy and attention to be realized in full.

Yes, nipping any sort of romantic notion between them in the bud was for the best.

Between bites, she glanced over and caught him watching her. The pair of chopsticks she held in her right hand stilled and she stopped chewing. She nearly stopped breathing, as, during one long, poignant moment, a pair of dark eyes took her measure.

What do you see?

She desperately wanted to ask him. She wanted to demand an answer if necessary. A host of other questions bubbled to the surface then, too.

When his lips tipped up in a smile that set off her pulse, the only one Emily didn't want answered was why she suddenly felt like crying.

CHAPTER SEVEN

IT WAS a nice evening for a walk, breezy and warm without a hint of humidity in the air. The meal they'd eaten, while far from being heavy, gave Madani another good excuse to ask Emily if she'd care to take a stroll after they left the restaurant.

Friends could do that, he told himself, even as the way he was admiring her legs had meandered into an arena well beyond the platonic.

"But what about Azeem?" She turned and glanced around. Neither the driver nor the Mercedes was anywhere to be found.

"He will come when I call for him."

And Madani hadn't called yet. He'd planned to just before they finished their main courses. That was usually what he did to give his driver enough time to arrive at the curb. But he'd procrastinated, not ready for his time with Emily to end. And once they were in his automobile, under Azeem's knowing eye, it would.

"He doesn't mind just waiting around for his phone to ring?" she asked.

"Not very much." Madani smiled, though, knowing that his good friend would indeed grumble mightily to him about it later. He always did.

Emily switched the small clutch she held to her other hand and turned slightly as they walked, giving him, rather than the antiques and curio shops, her undivided attention. "I get the feeling the two of you are more than just employee and employer."

"We are," he said simply.

"Is it difficult, being both his friend and his boss?" she asked.

"It can be difficult at times," he began. As the son of Kashaqra's ruler, Madani was used to people doing as he requested without hesitation let alone question. Azeem was the exception. Thinking of Azeem's opinion of Madani's betrothal contract, he continued,

"Azeem and I do not always agree, but he is one of the few people in my acquaintance who is not afraid to offer his true opinion even when he knows it will not be what I wish to hear. I respect him for that."

"You don't strike me as all that fearsome," Emily teased. "There must be another side to you I haven't seen."

If only she knew. Madani almost told her about his title then, just to discover if it would change the way she treated him. He hoped she would be like Azeem, able to see him first as a man and second as a ruler in waiting. But revealing his status chanced pulling his other secret out into the open. Though he had nothing to feel guilty about—Emily had initiated the kiss they'd shared earlier—he was enjoying her company too much. There was an ease, an intimacy to their conversation that surely would not exist were Emily privy to the upcoming announcement of his engagement.

She was saying, "Well, the fact Azeem speaks his mind around you makes him not only a friend, but a good one. I hope you appreciate his candor, even when what he says makes you uncomfortable or angry."

"Why do you say that?" Madani asked. Her tone, both wry and wistful, made him curious.

"Because I have a good friend—had, I guess, is the more accurate description at this point—who tried to tell me that Reed wasn't right for me. She tried to tell me that when push came to shove, he wouldn't be there for me. He wouldn't support my career. But I didn't listen to her." Emily lifted her shoulders. "I *wouldn't* listen."

"You did not want her to be right," he said, thinking of his arguments with Azeem on the betrothal agreement.

"Exactly. We argued about Reed on several occasions. I made excuses for his behavior. Excuses she shot full of holes. That in turn began to put a strain on our friendship. So, I started calling her less often." She motioned with her free hand. "Finding reasons I couldn't meet her for coffee or lunch. Then, finally, we both stopped picking up the phone. We haven't spoken in nearly three years."

"Obviously that troubles you. Why don't you call her now?" he asked.

"I'm embarrassed, I guess." Emily's

laughter was rueful. "Donna was absolutely right about Reed, and that was before he proved what an absolute jerk he was by running around with my sister behind my back."

"So, to avoid embarrassment you will deprive yourself of her friendship now?"

Emily wrinkled her nose. The gesture wasn't intended to be sexy. He found it to be so anyway. "When you put it like that it makes me sound foolish."

"I'm sorry. That wasn't my intent."

"No, don't apologize. You're right, Madani. One hundred percent correct. And I am being foolish. I've missed her so much," she said with feeling. "I have other friends, of course, but Donna and I go back a long way."

"If that is so, it won't matter the length of time that has passed. She will welcome hearing from you."

"Yeah." Emily nodded, slowly at first and then with vehemence. "She will. I'm going to call her. First thing tomorrow. Or maybe even when I get home tonight. Thank you."

"You're most welcome, though really I have done nothing."

"You're a good listener."

"I try to be." It was a trait his father reminded him often enough would serve him well as ruler.

Emily angled her head to one side. "Have you and Azeem ever not spoken?"

"No." Madani chuckled. "He is far too fond of talking to remain silent for any length of time."

"How long have you known him?"

"Since boyhood," he told her, and couldn't repress the smile the old memories teased out. "If I tell you that he can be a bad influence on me, will you think it the truth?"

"Perhaps," she replied diplomatically, but then her lips curved. "Although it seems highly unlikely."

Madani laughed outright. "My mother said the very thing when we were boys. Azeem's mother as well. Even when the mischief we got into was entirely of his making, he managed to escape all blame."

"*Entirely* of his making?"

"Mostly." At her raised eyebrows, he amended, "Well, at least in small part."

Her laughter rang out, surprisingly robust.

He liked hearing it. He liked seeing her looking so relaxed, especially after the afternoon she'd had. "It sounds as if they had you pegged."

"Pegged?" He turned the word over in his mind for a moment before understanding dawned. "Yes. I suppose they did."

"Besides, you don't strike me as the sort of person who would be easily led—even as a child and regardless of the temptation."

"No." He had not been easily led as child, nor as a man. Although he fought the urge, his gaze lowered to Emily's mouth, recalling the way it had felt against his. He swallowed hard. Temptation stood before him now in the form of a beautiful, sexy and exciting young woman. He wanted to know more of her, to know everything about her. He had neither the time nor the right. He glanced away, but because he could not completely curb his curiosity, he asked, "What sort of person do you think I am, Emily?"

"You're just fishing for compliments now," she accused on a laugh.

It was another unfamiliar phrase, but given the context of their conversation Madani figured it out easily enough. Chuckling, he said, "I suppose that I am. Will you be kind enough to indulge me?"

Emily's shoulders lifted in a shrug. "Why not?" But it was a moment before she went on, giving him the impression she was putting real thought into the exercise. "You come across as authoritative and very determined. It's clear that you know what you like and what you want."

"Yes." Indeed, he knew exactly what he liked, what he wanted. Not that he was free to do anything about it.

"I mean, white truffles, for heaven's sake." She blew out a breath and smiled. She was talking about food, which was just as well.

They reached a corner and, as they waited for the light to change, Emily continued. "I don't need to tell you that you're attractive. That night at the Hendersons', my assistant was sure you were a male underwear model."

He coughed. "That is a compliment, yes?"

"Oh, most definitely." She glanced around. "I'll point his ad out to you if I see one."

"I'll look forward to it," he said dryly.

She chuckled and, clearly enjoying his discomfort, went on. "You know, our waitress back at Fuwang's would have given me a serious case of food poisoning if she thought doing so would give her the chance to have you all to herself."

"You exaggerate."

She snorted. "She barely spared me a glance, even when I was ordering." Emily batted her long lashes at him. "She only had eyes for you, Madani."

"It is because I command attention." He said it tongue-in-cheek, even though from the cradle on his parents had taught him to be forceful, assertive.

"Right. You're also so humble," Emily deadpanned, drawing out his laughter. More seriously, she added, "You're obviously industrious and capable. You've created a very clever business opportunity for yourself. I think you're also generous, because your business opportunity in turn has offered the talented men and women of your homeland a way to market their wares overseas and make more money. In your own way, you're putting Kashaqra on the map."

Madani liked knowing Emily saw it that

way. It was what he'd intended, giving his people a better way to earn a living, encouraging a positive image abroad for his homeland.

"What else?"

"You're insatiable."

"Insatiable?" It was an interesting word choice, he thought, aware of its other meaning. And apropos, because when Madani was with Emily that was exactly how he felt: hungry for more and not just sexually.

In their relatively brief acquaintance he'd figured out a few things about her, such as while she came across as fiercely independent and driven, she was also vulnerable and surprisingly unsure of herself when it came to being a woman. Madani blamed her ex-boyfriend for that, though her family appeared to have had a hand in it as well. They'd given her either-or choices.

She could be smart or beautiful like her coddled younger sister. She could follow her dreams or she could have a husband. They'd made her choose when no choice was necessary and, in fact, making a choice had robbed her of a full and truly satisfying life.

Emily deserved better than that. She deserved…so much more.

A blush bloomed becomingly on her cheeks, the product, he assumed, of her unplanned double entendre. "I'm referring to your ego. It needs constant feeding. But then I've yet to meet a man whose ego doesn't."

He didn't care for the comparison, but Madani worked up a comically wounded expression as he placed his right hand over his heart. "Despite all of your flattery then, are you saying you find me mundane?"

"Oh, absolutely. That's the word that springs to mind. There's nothing new or original about you." Her lips curved with an unintentional invitation. It took all of Madani's willpower to resist.

"But you are original, Emily Merit, which is why I will remember our time together in Manhattan for the rest of my life."

He took her fingers in his. He meant only to give them a friendly squeeze. He and Emily were no longer in Chinatown. For that matter, Madani hadn't the slightest idea of where they were. But as he lifted the back of Emily's hand to his lips for a kiss, that wasn't why he was feeling so utterly lost.

"Oh my God!"

His gaze flew to hers, but she wasn't looking at him. She was staring over his shoulder, a combination of excitement and disbelief evident in her expression. The ego she'd just accused him of having deflated like a punctured balloon. Not that she noticed. She'd already pulled her hand from his and was hurrying toward the window of a nearby building.

"This is it!" she announced, turning to grin at him. "This is exactly the location I want and—oh, my God!—it's available right now."

He read the real estate sign tucked in the window, noted the ample square footage. "It seems large for a catering business." Not to mention pricey, he thought, especially when her remodeled kitchen could accommodate her needs.

"It's not for catering. It's for The Merit." She said it with a lofty inflection, pride and excitement beaming in her expression when she announced, "My restaurant."

* * *

Emily watched the words sink in and part of her braced, ready for a negative reaction, which was how Reed and even her family had greeted her plans to open her own eatery. Madani, however, nodded in approval and smiled.

"What kind of restaurant will it be? Tell me about it," he invited.

"That's the wrong thing to say." At his frown, she explained, "I can go on and on about the plans I have."

He merely shrugged. "I have the time."

A moment ago, when he'd kissed her hand, she'd nearly melted into a puddle of hormones. She'd considered staging a repeat of the scene in her mother's living room, might have followed through, too, had she not spied the For Lease sign in the window. Thankfully sanity had returned. It was threatening to flee again as he stood in front of her, by all appearances genuinely interested in hearing her expound on her dream.

"Are you sure?"

Madani glanced across the street to where a martini-glass-shaped neon sign blinked over the entrance of Dean's Place. A smattering of tables was set up on the sidewalk outside. He pointed to the lone empty one and said, "It's a nice evening to sit outside. Let me buy you a drink, and you can tell me all about your restaurant."

It was just after eleven when Emily and Madani left the bar. Although Madani objected, she paid their tab. It was the least she could do after everything the man had done for her this day.

The Mercedes was at the curb. By the time they reached the car, Azeem was holding open the rear door.

"I trust you had a good evening?" he inquired politely, although a bit of the devil gleamed in his gaze when he glanced Madani's way.

"We did."

"I hope we didn't ruin yours," Emily added.

"Ah, Miss Merit, you are too beautiful to ruin anything."

"If you're going to be so outrageous with your flattery, you must call me Emily."

"Emily." He nodded. "Where shall I take you now?"

"Home, please."

Madani rattled off the address and a moment later they were on their way.

Seated next to Madani, she wondered how it was possible to feel exhausted and energized at the same time. She already had a million ideas for her restaurant, ideas she'd typed into her computer and referenced on a regular basis, adding to them, weeding out those that wouldn't work, using them as a pick-me-up on those days when her outlook needed bolstering.

Tonight, she'd come up with even more ideas. Despite the late hour, they were popping around in her head like pinballs. Some of them had come courtesy of Madani. The man was an excellent listener and sounding board. She appreciated his advice and the respectful way in which he offered it. Whenever Reed had given Emily suggestions, he'd made her feel like a dim-witted child for not having thought of them first.

As the car pulled to the curb, she held up the cocktail napkin on which she had jotted down some notes.

"Thank you." She waved the napkin. "For

this and for everything else. I'm in your debt."

He shook his head. "Never."

"I enjoyed myself tonight. It's been a long time since I've gone out and let someone else do the cooking." Her laughter was rueful.

"You should do it more often."

"It's hard to find the time."

"You should make the time."

"All work and no play…" She'd said the same thing at her parent's house. At his frown, she added, "It's a saying. All work and no play makes Jack a dull boy. Or, in my case, Emily. And, well, it makes me a dull girl." She was babbling. It was the way he was looking at her.

"You're much too interesting to ever be considered dull, Emily."

She tried to laugh, but the sound that escaped was more of a sigh.

"Well, I'd better go." Before she could reach for the door, however, Azeem hopped out from the driver's seat and opened it for her.

Madani followed her. "I'll walk you up," he said.

"Oh, that's not necessary."

"Indulge me."

Azeem said something to Madani then in their native language. Even in the low light cast by the streetlamps, Emily could see Madani flush. If his terse-sounding reply was any indication, in addition to being embarrassed, he was irritated.

Azeem, however, was unperturbed. Indeed, he laughed robustly. "Of course, my friend. But you are a fool."

Since Azeem had switched back to English, Madani did as well. "I will return in no more than five minutes." The words were said slowly and enunciated with care.

"No more than five minutes? A man should never admit to that."

Madani slipped back into his language for his reply and his inflection made it clear he'd just said something that could not be repeated in polite company.

"Is everything all right?" she asked when they stepped into her building's elevator a moment later. "Between you and Azeem, I mean."

"Fine."

Though it wasn't like her to pry, Emily said, "It didn't sound fine. And I can't help feeling I'm somehow responsible for the exchange."

"No. You did not cause our words."

"Maybe I didn't cause them, but you were talking about me. Weren't you, Madani?"

"Yes." He glanced away, sighed. "I apologize for both of us."

She pulled a face, seeking to lighten the moment. "Gee, was what you said about me *that* rude?"

He found no humor in her question. "No. Rest assured that Azeem has nothing but respect for you, as do I."

"But," she prompted.

"As I already mentioned, my friend can be quite outspoken in expressing his opinions. I have certain obligations, duties," he said softly. "I take them very seriously. I must. Azeem…we differ on how I should approach those obligations."

"If that was intended as an explanation, I'm afraid I'm still in the dark." She laughed awkwardly. Obligations. Duties. For the first time it struck her how little she knew about the man.

A bell dinged as the elevator reached her floor. She stepped into the empty hallway when the doors parted. Madani remained in the car. His gaze was intense. The way he dragged a hand through his hair hinted at frustration.

"Emily, I want you to know that…"

"Yes?"

"I wish…"

The doors started to close. They both reached out to stop them. "What do you wish?"

He blinked, smiled charmingly and let his hands drop. The turmoil she'd glimpsed just a moment before was gone from his expression.

"I wish you a good night."

CHAPTER EIGHT

"Who is he?"

Emily's sister demanded this even before offering a proper greeting as she waltzed into Emily's apartment late the following morning.

Despite a poor night's sleep, Emily had been in a terrific mood. First thing upon waking, she'd followed through on her promise to reconnect with her friend. She'd gotten Donna's voice mail, left a message. An hour ago, Donna had returned Emily's call and agreed to meet with her for drinks the following week. The conversation had been brief and on the awkward side. Emily had expected no less given the passage of time and the old hurts. But it was a start. Her good mood leached away with Elle's unexpected appearance.

"Hello to you, too," she muttered and closed the door with enough force to leave the locks rattling. "Just in the neighborhood?" If so, she would have to see about moving.

Whereas Emily was pretty sure she looked like the last one standing after a cafeteria food fight—her apron was splattered with the ingredients of the half dozen recipes she'd worked on since dawn—Elle was fresh and radiant in a pale pink linen suit whose three-quarter-length sleeves offered an unrestricted view of the diamond bracelet Reed had given her to mark their engagement.

"Actually I sort of was. I'm meeting Reed at Herman's for lunch in an hour." Elle set her luggage-size Gucci bag on one of the stools lined up in front of the granite-topped island and sighed dramatically. "We're going over song selections for our first dance."

"Gee, that could take hours," Emily replied.

The sarcasm sailed over her sister's bleached-blond head. "I know, but he only can spare one. He's a busy and important man."

Which was why Reed wanted—*required*—

a woman who had an open schedule so she could drop everything when he had a free moment to spend with her. With her restaurant dreams to pursue and a catering business to run, Emily had been a square peg to his round hole. Not so Elle. She and Reed complemented one another perfectly.

"Are you here to ask me for suggestions?" If so, Emily had some, though none was a song title.

"No. I thought we could…chat. We hardly had a moment to spend together yesterday at my shower." Elle shook her heavy cascade of blonde curls. The color was manufactured, but the texture was natural. Though Emily hated herself for it, she found herself fingering the ends of her stick-straight brown hair.

"So, who is he?" Elle asked a second time.

"Who is who?"

Her sister folded her arms over her chest, creating more impressive cleavage in the linen jacket. "Don't play dumb, Em. We both know I'm referring to the man you practically mauled in Mom's living room. It was all any of the aunts could talk about for the rest of the afternoon."

Indignation paired with embarrassment had Emily shooting back, "I didn't maul him. It was a kiss."

"It was more than a kiss and we both know it." Elle held up her diamond-heavy left hand to forestall Emily's retort. "Hey, I'm not finding fault. He's a yummy specimen. If my wedding to Reed wasn't just a couple of months away, I would be tempted to sample him, too."

Emily's mouth gaped open for a moment. Was it sheer nerve that caused her backstabbing baby sister to make that comment or could Elle really be that oblivious to its poor taste?

"Well?" Elle demanded when Emily remained silent. "Are you going to give me details or not?"

As if she was entitled to them? Em gritted her teeth. She needed something to do with her hands…before she used them to strangle her way to only-child status. She put the kitchen island between them, picked up the citrus zester and grabbed a lemon from the bowl on the countertop. With a bit more force than necessary, she shaved tiny bits of yellow peel into what was to become a marinade for a chicken recipe.

Cooking. It was her savior.

"Madani is a client, but we also enjoy one another's company." What she said was the truth, though for some reason she wanted to sigh with regret.

"I thought his name was Dan?"

"Dan. Yes. Short for Madani."

"Madani?" Elle repeated. "What's his last name?"

"Tarim."

"Madani Tarim." Elle's perfectly arched brows drew together. "Why does that sound familiar?"

"I can't imagine. Maybe one of the characters on your soap opera shares it."

Elle puckered her lips thoughtfully, but shook her head a moment later. "No. That's not it. But I've heard it somewhere and recently I think."

"I'll take your word for it." Emily dipped the tip of her index finger in the marinade for a taste and added another pinch of salt.

"Mom said you gave her the impression nothing was going on between the two of you." She snorted then. "Aunt Sally said if that was nothing, then every single woman in New York should be so lucky."

Emily resisted the urge to fan herself. Instead, she shrugged. "You know how Mom is. It's never a good idea to give her too much information."

"Is he…an escort?"

"What?" The word came out more shout than question.

"I'd understand completely if you—you know—had to hire a man to fill certain voids in your life. We all need…companionship."

Companionship. It was code for sex and they both knew it. Apparently Elle had counted up the months she'd been with Reed and deduced that Emily hadn't enjoyed a good, sweaty bout between the sheets since then. It stunk that her sister was half right. Emily had lived like a novitiate since then. Though truth be told she'd never found sex with Reed—who'd been her first and only lover—to be all that mind-blowing. She thought it was her. Maybe she just wasn't all that sexual. She knew better now that she'd met Madani. With a mere kiss on the back of her hand he'd caused a more intense physical reaction than Reed could muster with half an hour of inventive foreplay.

Still, Emily was outraged that her sister thought her to be so desperate and unappealing that she needed to pay for sexual fulfillment.

"Madani Tarim is not on my payroll in any way, shape or form," she snapped.

"Jeez, Em." Elle held up both hands. "There's no need to get so worked up."

"I'm not worked up. I'm insulted, Elle. Even you should be able to figure out why."

"Fine." Her sister rolled her baby blues skyward. "I'm sorry."

Yeah, she sounded sorry. Emily decided to let it go. "Forget it."

"So, is it serious?"

Emily chose her words carefully, well aware that every single one of them, in some fashion or another, would be relayed to her entire extended family. "I don't know that I'd call it serious. We're good friends."

"Good friends, hmm?" Elle's smile turned

sly. "Is that another way of saying friends with benefits?"

The innuendo had heat flaring in Emily's cheeks. The topic just kept coming back to sex and, for a woman who had lain awake half the night thinking about it, she didn't need this now.

"Aren't you just full of questions this morning?" she evaded frostily.

"We're sisters."

"A fact that you tend to recall only when it's convenient for you."

Elle glanced away. "Come on, Em. I'm worried about you, okay? It's been months since you last came to a family dinner at Mom and Pop's."

"Three guesses why."

Elle ignored the jab and went on. "Given your crazy work schedule you can't have much time to go out with friends on weekends."

"I like my job."

"And I'd bet my favorite pair of Jimmy Choos that you haven't gone on a date since…"

"Since Reed?"

Elle moistened her lips. "Yes."

Emily set the zester aside and stared at her sister over the span of the island. "Are you feeling a little guilty?"

Emily wanted her sister to be. More than that, she wanted the apology that was long overdue. Perhaps then she would be able truly to put the sordid mess behind her and move on. She, Reed and Elle would never be one big happily dysfunctional family, sitting down to Sunday dinner at her folks' house, but an apology would help.

Elle didn't apologize, though. She crossed her arms and pouted. And it stunk that her sister could look so damned good doing something so childish.

"God, Em! You're so mean. Do you have to dredge that up again? Can't we move on already? It's been a year." Tears worked their way to the edges of Elle's baby blues, but her face remained splotchless and amazingly her eye makeup remained perfectly in place.

I've got to learn how to cry like that, Em thought.

"Gee, sorry. I don't know what I was thinking." Except, how like her sister to flip the situation around, turn herself into the victim and wangle an apology out of Emily.

Emily picked up the zester and went to work on the lemon again.

"I just want you to find someone who makes you feel as special as I do whenever I'm with Reed."

I thought I had. It took an effort for Emily to bite her tongue and she was glad she had, because she realized now, it wasn't true. Reed hadn't made her feel special. He'd made her feel…inadequate and even intractable for wanting to pursue her own dreams rather than help him pursue his.

"What we have together, it's such a fairy tale," Elle was saying. "You know like Romeo and Julia."

"Juliet," Em corrected.

"Right." She waved a hand dismissively. "Her."

The dreamy sigh that ensued had the same effect on Emily's nerves as fingernails being scratched down a chalkboard. Maybe she should point out that in Shakespeare's play the young, star-crossed lovers had both wound up dead.

She didn't. What was the point? Instead, she asked in exasperation, "How is it possible that we're sisters?"

Elle stared blankly.

"We have the same parents," Emily said. "In many cases we had the same opportunities."

Elle continued to stare blankly.

"How is it possible for us to be such polar opposites? And I don't just mean in looks. I'm willing to work for what I want. You…you expect everyone else to do the heavy lifting for you. And do you know what stinks about that? They do. Mom and Dad have always given you a free pass."

Elle's expression went from blank to wounded. "I'm sorry that you've always been so jealous of me, Em. It's not my fault that my life has worked out so well while yours is so empty."

"Empty." She thought of her catering business, the satisfaction she'd felt watching it grow. And her plans for the restaurant, which continued to inch closer to reality. "Is that what you think?"

"Reed says—"

"Don't!" Emily held the zester out like a

weapon. "I don't want to hear Reed's opinion of my life. I heard it too often when we were dating. Besides, we're talking about you. You're smart, Elle. You could do anything, *be* anything, if you just started applying yourself. Don't you have any ambitions?"

"Of course I do." She gave her hair an indignant toss. "I want to become Mrs. Reed Benedict in a wedding that will be the talk of the town for years to come."

Emily closed her eyes and sighed. They were back at square one.

"At least I'm not going to wind up old and alone." Elle raised her hand. "I don't want to fight. That's not why I came here today."

"No, you wanted to find out if I'd hired a male escort."

"I was hoping you'd found someone special to bring to my wedding," Elle said coolly. "I still haven't received your RSVP."

"That's because I haven't decided if I'm coming—alone or otherwise."

"But you have to come," Elle all but wailed. "You have to be a bridesmaid." Her genuine disappointment might have caused

Emily to waver had she not added, "If you don't agree to stand up I'll be forced to have our cousin Constance in the wedding party, and she's put on so much weight since she got married."

Emily gaped. "Constance just had a baby, Elle."

"Hello. Three months ago. And at the slow rate she's losing the weight, she's still going to be at least a size eight in August."

"Tragedy," Emily muttered.

Elle ignored her. "Besides, the peach organdy I picked out does nothing for her complexion."

Emily had seen the dress. Nothing about its color or cut did anything for any of the bridesmaids' complexions and figures. But then, that was why Elle had chosen it.

"Say you'll think about it," she implored.

Because agreeing with her sister was easier than listening to her whine, Emily nodded.

"Great!" Elle clapped her hands together in childish delight before her expression turned calculating. "So, will you bring your new man to the wedding? Mom and the aunts are dying to corner him and pry out every last detail of his life. You should have heard the way they went on and on about him yesterday after you left."

Emily didn't need to have heard them. She could imagine the conversations perfectly. So, her relationship with the sexy and mysterious Dan was the subject of family speculation and gossip. That was just what she'd hoped for when she'd planted that kiss on him. Objective achieved.

So why didn't she like it?

Her grip tightened on the zester. "I don't think I'll be bringing him. I wouldn't want to put him through that."

Besides, long before Reed and Elle celebrated their first dance as husband and wife, Madani would be back in his homeland. Emily's heart gave a funny thump at the thought. She passed it off as regret. After all, the kiss apparently had left the impression with the Poor Emily crowd that she was having a good old time post-Reed. Once they learned the affair had gone nowhere—and given the efficiency of the Merit family grapevine, they would hear it before Madani's plane lifted off the runway—her first name once again would be preceded by a pity-garnering qualifier.

Elle frowned. "Oh. So you'll be coming solo."

"I haven't said I will be coming at all."

"Em," her sister wailed. "You've got to."

"Because I'll look better in the dress than Constance?" Emily nearly laughed.

"Of course not." Elle nibbled her lip. "But you will. Besides, I've paired you with Grant Barrymore. You know him."

Yes, she knew him. She also detested him. Reed and Grant were longtime friends. They had pledged the same fraternity in college, making them "brothers." But that hadn't stopped Grant from making a pass at Emily one night when he'd had too much to drink.

Wasn't anyone capable of loyalty or restraint anymore? Was Emily the only one who valued honesty and believed trust to be the foundation of a relationship?

Madani. The name and thoughts of the man blasted free from her subconscious.

He would, Emily decided. Any man who would let a woman kiss him the way Emily had and later the same evening leave her at the doorstep would understand restraint.

If Emily were in the market for a man, Madani would be exactly the sort she would fall for fast and hard. Good thing she wasn't in the market.

"Is that going to be edible?"

Elle's question brought her back to the present. She blinked at her sister. "Wh-what?"

"Whatever it is you're making. It doesn't look very appetizing." Elle's nose wrinkled.

Emily glanced down at the pulpy remains of the lemon clutched in her hand. She'd grated off every last bit of the peel and most of the bitter white pith. The marinade was ruined. She would have to start over.

Emily was on Madani's mind, starting with a sleepless Sunday night through the rest of the week. The more time he spent with her the more he wanted to spend with her. Add in that kiss and his mind was straying to forbidden places.

Friendship. It was what he'd offered her as they'd dined in Fuwang's. It was what he'd shown her later, when he listened intently to her plans for a restaurant.

Friendship. He'd never been friends with a woman before. Friendly, but not actual friends. He wanted so much more from Emily. But it was all he had to offer.

Sleep with her.

That was Azeem's unhelpful suggestion. He thought Madani should engage in a brief but mutually satisfying affair, maybe buy her a lovely trinket at the end of it. That way he would get Emily Merit and all women out of his system while he was still entitled to do so. He'd said so again Sunday evening—though thankfully in Arabic—when they'd arrived outside Emily's apartment.

Even after Madani had returned to the car—a full two minutes shy of the five minutes he'd predicted—his friend had continued goading him.

"I don't understand you. Why are you here with me when a young and beautiful woman is alone in her rooms and undressing as we speak?"

"Shut up and drive."

"Your mood would improve dramatically

if you allowed yourself to relieve some frustration. I can turn the car around at the next light and take you back. I doubt she would mind the intrusion."

"No."

But his friend had continued as if Madani hadn't spoken. "In fact, from the way she looked at you tonight, I think she would welcome the intrusion."

"I said no."

"I could return for you in the morning, though not too early." He'd turned and winked. "You will have good reason to sleep late."

"Enough!" Madani had shouted as erotic images reeled through his mind.

Given the fierceness of both his tone and expression, he'd figured his friend would back down at the command, maybe even apologize for having gone too far. He should have known better. Azeem snickered and not at all discreetly.

"At dinner tonight Emily asked me if it was difficult to be both your employer and your friend. I warn you, Azeem. If you keep it up I will be neither."

"Your threats would hold more weight,

sadiqi, if I thought you actually meant them." He smiled, unperturbed. "We have known one another far too long."

"I was just thinking the same thing." Madani shoved a hand through his hair and exhaled loudly.

"You are not angry with me. You are angry with yourself."

"It is done, Azeem. How many times must I say it?"

"No. The engagement has not been officially announced. Your father will listen to you. He is a reasonable man, hardly provincial in his views. He has ushered much change into Kashaqra, brought our people into a new century."

"He honors the old ways."

"You are being a fool."

"Don't go there. Not again. Or at least not tonight." He'd rubbed his eyes, suddenly exhausted. "I am too tired for more verbal sparring."

"Because you know I am right," Azeem had said. In a more thoughtful tone, he'd asked, "Or perhaps someone else has started to change your mind?"

Now, four days later, Madani mulled his friend's words as he sat on the terrace of his apartment at The Mark drinking a cup of the sweetened black coffee favored in his homeland. More than a dozen stories below, the midday traffic buzzed along on Madison Avenue, the blaring horns muted by distance and his own distraction.

If he thought a brief but satisfying affair with Emily Merit would get her out of his system he might have allowed Azeem to turn the car around that evening. There was no denying he was physically attracted to her and had been since their introduction in the Hendersons' kitchen. At each meeting during the two weeks since then his desire for her had only increased. As had his interest beyond the physical. That was the real problem.

He liked Emily, truly enjoyed her company. He admired her determination, the dreams she'd so carefully nurtured and refused to give up even in the face of adversity and heartache. She was amusing, thoughtful and incredibly bright. Not just a beautifully wrapped package like her younger sister, but one filled with riches and substance. Madani wanted to spend the next several weeks, even months, getting to know her better. He didn't have that luxury. Precious little time remained of either his visit to New York or of his bachelorhood.

One week after his dinner party Madani would return home. A month after that all of Kashaqra would mark the start of The Feast of Seven Days, which celebrated the country's overthrow of an oppressive ruler. As the celebration wound down his engagement would be announced.

His future was set.

He drained the last of his coffee. As sweet as it was, it turned bitter in his mouth. For as long as Madani could remember, whatever he'd wanted he'd gotten. Thanks to his wealth and rank, nothing ever had been beyond his reach.

Until now.

CHAPTER NINE

WITH two events on Merit Catering's schedule for the following day, Emily's kitchen was a beehive of activity Friday evening, and it had been since midafternoon.

At the island, Arlene was mixing up the crab meat filling that would be piped into pastry puffs and baked on location at the birthday party in Connecticut. All five layers of the cake had been baked and were cooling on the counter. The raspberry mousse filling was mixed and chilling in the refrigerator.

Emily had just returned from her favorite gourmet market for the last of the ingredients for Madani's dinner, including the fresh herbs and pricey white truffles. She'd planned to shop with Madani, but scheduling conflicts forced her to go solo.

Setting her shopping bag on the counter, she dipped her index finger into the bowl for a taste. "I think it needs a little more Worcestershire."

"I like it with less," Arlene said.

"I like it with more."

"And you're the boss."

It was an old argument, so Emily laughed.

Arlene grabbed the bottle of Worcestershire. As she added a few more dashes to the mix, she grumbled. "A bunch of bratty five-year-olds aren't going to care."

"No, but their parents might be more discerning when it comes to crab tarts. And if they like them the way Merit Catering makes them, they might hire us to do an adult event in the future."

"Pay attention, Sarita," Arlene said to the young culinary arts student who'd been helping out for the afternoon.

Emily regularly employed students from her alma mater, making up in on-the-job experience what she couldn't afford to give them in actual pay. She was grateful for the added help this day, even if the young woman had an endless supply of questions that kept breaking the rhythm Emily and Arlene had down to a science.

A knock sounded at the door as Emily carefully unpacked the truffles.

"Can you get that, Sarita? It's probably a delivery. I'm expecting some wine."

Even though Madani said he had everything he needed for his party, she'd picked up a couple of bottles of a special vintage for him. They were a thank-you of sorts not only for rescuing her from her sister's bridal shower but for listening so thoughtfully as she'd expounded on her restaurant plans.

"Um, Miss Merit," Sarita called a moment later. "It's for you."

She glanced over and her gaze locked with Madani's. His smile was slightly embarrassed, and all the sexier for it.

"I am catching you at a bad time," he said.

"No." Her palms felt damp. She wiped them on her apron. "I mean, yes. But come in."

Arlene cleared her throat noisily and mumbled, "An introduction would be nice."

"Oh. Right. Madani Tarim, this is my assistant, Arlene." Emily pointed to the other young woman. "And that's Sarita."

"Ladies."

He smiled. They sighed. Emily wanted to groan.

"So, what brings you by?" she asked.

"I brought some wine for you to try."

"That's funny," she said, thinking of the wine she'd ordered for him.

"Funny?"

Emily waved a hand. "Never mind."

"I planned to serve this tomorrow evening, but I wanted your opinion first. I wouldn't want it to clash with the menu you've so carefully planned." He held out the bottle for her inspection.

Emily read the label. She recognized the name of the French winery. The bottle hadn't come cheaply. In fact, it cost double what hers had. But that didn't surprise her. Madani wasn't the sort of man to go halfway. "This was an excellent year for pinot noir, I believe. It should pair well with the fish."

"Care for a glass?" he asked. His gaze included the others.

"Now?" Emily glanced back at the kitchen where so much remained to be done. Even so, she shrugged. "I suppose a taste wouldn't hurt."

"I'll get the glasses." Arlene grinned.

Sarita was still staring at Madani with unabashed adoration. It was embarrassing, but understandable. Emily liked looking at him herself. She cleared her throat. "Arlene, grab four glasses from the cupboard. I think we've all earned a few minutes of downtime."

Two hours later the wine was gone. Sarita was, too, having left after half a glass to meet friends who'd called from a pub on Bleecker. Arlene was preparing to leave as well since she would be back early the next morning to wrap things up and load the catering van. She had finished the appetizers for the birthday party and done what prep work could be done for the entrées.

Madani was the only one who showed no interest in leaving. Not that Emily minded. It was no hardship to spend time with him. He'd watched the food preparation with interest, asking lots of questions that made it clear he'd never boiled water much less decorated a birthday cake, which Emily started on after Arlene left.

"This isn't exactly my forte," she admitted as she began spreading the raspberry mousse between layers of white cake. "I explained that to my client. In fact, I gave her the name of a bakery I do a lot of business with. But, she insisted."

"She must have faith in you."

"I think she just wanted to write one check and be done with it. She's a *very busy woman*," Emily intoned. "She must have told me that every time we spoke. It kind of made me wonder why she wanted to have a child." She added another layer of cake. "I'm busy, too. Probably busier than she is since Babs knows her and said she doesn't have a paying job. But I know my limits and I've determined my priorities."

"Are you saying you will never marry and have children?" Madani asked quietly.

The blunt question, which came just as Emily was leveling the second layer, caught her off-guard. She stopped midcut and glanced over at him. He was watching her closely.

"I won't say never, but it's looking doubtful. And since I see parenting as a two-person job, I probably won't be having kids."

Emily had made peace with the fact that her career plans were incompatible with a long-term relationship and parental responsibilities. Or she thought she had. But saying so now to Madani caused a dull throbbing to begin in her chest. She'd thought it a fair trade, but now she felt cheated.

"Is your decision based on what happened with Benedict?" he asked.

"Yes and no." She finished trimming the layer and set the blade aside. "The reality is, I work a lot of nights and most weekends. Reed didn't want me to succeed at my career for a variety of reasons, my schedule included."

Madani spat out something in his native tongue. Given the sharpness of his tone, she didn't need to ask for a translation. Her lips tipped up. "Yeah, I know. Reed's a first-class jerk."

"The phrase I came up with was a little more descriptive," Madani replied dryly. "He's intimidated by your success. It makes him feel like less of a man."

She smiled fully. "I realize that now. It takes some of the sting out of the fact that he cheated on me and with my sister."

"He didn't deserve you, Emily."

Her smile faded. He said it with such sincerity, with such utter authority, that she wanted to cry. She exhaled slowly instead and admitted the truth. "He was right about one thing, though. I'm pretty much married to my work and I will be for the foreseeable future."

"Even when you open The Merit?" he asked.

When, he'd said. Not *if.* The ache in her chest went from dull to piercing. Madani believed in her. He understood that her restaurant was no more a whim than catering was a hobby.

"Especially then. At least at first. Control freak, remember?" She laughed tightly. "What about you? Your job involves a lot of travel. That has to be hard on relationships."

It occurred to Emily that even though she felt she knew Madani so well, she was clueless when it came to his personal life. He could be involved with someone. Involved, hell. For all she knew, he could have a wife and kids back in Kashaqra. No, she told herself. He would have mentioned them before now, especially after that kiss. Even so, she held her breath as she waited for his reply.

"I wouldn't know."

She had no right to the relief she felt. Nor did she have a right to ask, "Do you think you'll marry one day and start a family?"

"Yes. I will marry." His tone was resolute and oddly grim. His expression bordered on bleak.

"No need to sound so happy about it," she teased, hoping to lighten his mood.

But he sounded every bit as ominous when he replied, "I will do what must be done." That was all he offered on the topic before changing subjects. "Have you called on the building for your restaurant?"

She'd been so excited about it the other night she'd wanted to telephone the real estate company right away. Only the fact it had been a Sunday evening had stopped her. By Monday morning, reality had tempered her excitement. She was in no position to buy or lease the space, which meant she had no business wasting a real estate agent's time.

"No. It will be a good year before I've saved up enough money to approach the bank and expect someone in the loan department to take me seriously."

He frowned. "What about investors?"

She scooped up the filling and began spreading it atop the cake layer. "I've considered that route. The Hendersons even said they would stake me, but I'd rather the risk be all mine. Well, mine and the bank's." She shrugged.

He frowned. "But the building, you said it was the perfect location and the square footage ideal."

Yes, she'd said that and still felt that way, which only made it more difficult to resist calling for details and requesting to see the inside.

"It is the perfect location for The Merit and I loved the building's architecture. But the timing is off." She laid the spatula aside and sighed. "I almost wish I hadn't found it. Knowing it's there, available and I can't have it makes it harder, you know?"

"I do. Exactly." His gaze was intense, tortured. "I, too, have found something special. Something I want very badly and cannot have." He reached over to tuck the hair that had escaped her ponytail behind her ear. Almost to himself he murmured, "Yet I cannot stay away."

Emily's mouth went dry at the same time her knees turned to liquid. No, he couldn't mean…

"You'll be leaving soon," she said softly. "Maybe being back in Kashaqra will help you forget whatever it is."

But he shook his head. "It will not matter where I am. Here or half a world away." His throat worked a moment before he confessed, "I will still want to be with you."

"Madani—"

"I want you, Emily. It is as simple as that and as complicated."

He closed the scant distance between them. When his hands framed her face, she closed her eyes. *Tell him to go,* she thought. *Tell him to stop.* She said nothing at all, instead luxuriated in his touch and waited for the moment their mouths would meet. When they did, she moaned. Her reasons for steering clear of men were sound, but they didn't negate basic need. That's what this was, she assured herself. Sexual need. It was building inside her now, like the cake she had been carefully erecting layer upon layer under Madani's watchful eye.

Thanks to hard work and sacrifice, she had a thriving catering business. One day, she would open her restaurant. But right now what Emily wanted, what she craved above all else, was this man.

In her mother's living room, their passionate kiss had been for show. Because of their audience, when it had ended, all of their clothing had been intact and their hands in politically correct places.

Well, no one was watching them now.

The kiss deepened. In the privacy of her apartment, Emily gave in to temptation. Her hands strayed from the safety of his shoulders and trailed across the firm expanse of his chest. Beneath one palm, she could feel his heart beating, the cadence fast and strong. Heat radiated from him and spiraled through her. All the while, the kiss went on. It was thrilling, maddening. By far the best kiss she'd ever experienced. Even so, Emily was determined to have more.

She clutched the soft fabric of his shirt in her hands, wrinkling it even as she contemplated ripping it. No doubt it was designer label, and as such obscenely expensive. The thought had her refraining. Her fingers found the placket of buttons instead and she began weaving one after the other through the hole.

By the time the task was complete Madani had started one of his own. As his mouth cruised across her cheek and then down her neck, he untied her apron and tossed it aside. Free of that layer, he tugged the hem of her shirt from her skirt. The shirt was a conservative pullover, beneath which she was wearing an equally conservative bra. It seemed an eternity before she was divested of the former. She helped him out of his as well, pushing the fabric down his arms and took a moment to admire his form. Madani was beautiful. Physical perfection. And the way he was looking at her made Emily feel the same. A forgotten part of her reveled in the sensation. She'd always been confident as a chef. As a woman, she'd questioned herself. Madani's frank appreciation, though, had her stopping the unhealthy practice. For that alone she would remember this man, this moment, for the rest of her life.

Then she was in his arms, hot skin

pressed to hot skin, and coherent thought once again fled.

"Emily." Madani moaned and then mumbled something unintelligible.

She understood perfectly.

Even though they were in the kitchen, her bedroom was mere steps away. But the countertop just behind her was much closer. As if he'd read her mind, he lifted her onto it, changing the dynamics considerably. Emily was half a head taller than he was now, and she liked where his gaze was drawn.

When it came to her figure, she wasn't voluptuous, but she filled out a bra well enough. Too bad the one she had on was plain white cotton and came from a department store. Had she anticipated their encounter, she would have made sure to be wearing one of the silk and lace numbers she'd bought a few years back at a pricey boutique.

She decided lingerie was overrated when he leaned closer and deftly undid the fastener. She felt the heat of his breath and then the heat his breath inspired. Either eventually would have stoked the mercury into triple digits on a thermometer. Together they accomplished the task handily. She was going to combust soon. She simply didn't care. In fact, she was eager to give herself over to the flames.

With the hope of improving his access, she levered backward. She intended to lay her palms flat on the counter for support. Unfortunately one of them wound up in the bowl of raspberry mousse, the other in the side of the not-quite-finished cake. Just that quickly reality inserted itself. Emily issued an oath and straightened. She had no business kissing him, let alone working her way to complete satisfaction. Madani was sexy, smart, fascinating and kind, but he was a client. Besides, she knew all to well that certain ingredients didn't mix well with her career.

"I'm sorry." She whispered it.

"Perhaps I am the one who should apologize. Your dessert is ruined," he said softly.

He retrieved a damp dishcloth from the sink and handed it to her, averting his gaze as Emily wiped up her hands and then fumbled for her bra. The moment was as ruined as the dessert, and they both knew it.

He grabbed his crumpled shirt off the floor along with Emily's. She waited until they were both fully dressed before saying, "I have to get back to work."

"Yes." He nodded toward the smashed cake. "And now you have more of it."

"I don't mind." It was a lousy thing to say given the circumstances. Oddly, he nodded and looked almost relieved himself.

They walked in silence to the door. It was a dozen steps of pure torture during which Emily nearly asked him to stay. Forget work. Forget the cake. She could buy one in the morning. But that was only putting off the inevitable. They had no future. She'd known that before things got out of hand.

"I'm sorry, Madani. I've acted very unprofessionally," she began.

He laid a finger across her lips. "No. I am the one who should apologize. I took advantage of the situation. I had no right." He glanced away, his tone more fierce when he repeated, "I had no right."

Ashamed of his behavior and aching for something that went far beyond sex, Madani slammed out of Emily's apartment. He took the stairs rather than waiting for the elevator. As he stalked across the lobby to the exit he marveled that he hadn't broken his neck given the reckless speed at which he had descended. But he'd had to get away from her before he gave in to desire, capitulated to primal instinct and committed the unforgivable.

Azeem wasn't waiting at the curb. Madani realized too late that he hadn't given his friend a time to return. Nor had he called for him. He would have to do that, but not just yet. He needed to think. And so he began walking, aimlessly at first and then with a destination in mind. An hour and a couple of phone calls later, he was standing outside the building Emily loved when the Mercedes pulled up. Azeem's amused smile melted away the instant Madani climbed into the front passenger seat.

"What has happened?" he asked.

"Nothing."

"You are talking to me, *sadiqi*. What has happened?"

"Not nearly enough." Madani laughed

harshly, though that wasn't why his throat ached afterward. "I shouldn't have gone to see her tonight. I don't know what I was thinking." Through the car's window, he studied the building, recalling what Emily had said earlier that evening about finding what she wanted at the wrong time. "In some ways I wish I'd never met her."

He half expected his friend to start in again with an argument about bucking the marriage arrangement his parents had brokered on his behalf so long ago. But Azeem replied enigmatically, "I know exactly how you feel."

The remainder of their drive to The Mark was accomplished in silence.

CHAPTER TEN

FOR THE FIRST TIME in her professional life Emily considered standing up a client.

How could she face Madani after last night? She'd kissed him in abandon, stripped him of his shirt and then allowed him to return the favor. If she hadn't leaned back and put her hands in raspberry mousse and white cake, they would have made love. She wanted to be grateful that sanity had returned before the deed was done, but gratitude hadn't managed to navigate past her still tangled-up hormones. It would have been really, really good sex. And she hadn't had sex of any sort in a very long time.

The irony of the situation wasn't lost on Emily, either. Her job had, in a very literal sense, again proved incompatible with romance. Business needed to be her priority, her focus. Not a man and a relationship that had no chance of succeeding.

After he'd gone, she'd baked more cakes and mixed up more filling. She barely managed a few hours of restless sleep before her alarm went off the following morning. Thus, it was no surprise she was in a foul mood and not operating up to speed. Her hastily reconstructed layer cake was leaning like the famed tower in Pisa, Italy.

Arlene came in as Emily finished the last sickly looking rosebud.

"That's…" Noting Emily's dark expression, her assistant angled her head to one side and proclaimed, "Nice. Very nice."

Emily tossed the bag of frosting onto the counter. "Go ahead and say it. It's off. I'm off. Nothing is going according to plan."

She wasn't only talking about the cake. Madani's face flashed in her mind. She could pretend she was disappointed and out of sorts because they hadn't had sex, but the truth was, it went deeper than that. As foolish as it was, she kept trying to figure out

a way they could work around her crazy
hours and his visitor status.

She wanted to cry then and it must have
showed. Arlene reached over and gave her
shoulders a quick squeeze. "Don't sweat it,
Em. I'll call Tiffany at Cakes for Every
Occasion. She's bound to have something
that will work for a kid's birthday party."

Yes, Tiffany would save the day, but
Emily was starting to fear there would be no
saving her heart.

At twenty minutes to five, she sucked up
her pride and packed Arlene's car with everything she would need for Madani's meal.
Emily had given her assistant use of the van
since the party in Connecticut was much
larger.

"Ready or not," she murmured upon
reaching her destination.

She'd never catered a party at The Mark
and she couldn't help but be impressed when
she was ushered up to Madani's gorgeously
appointed Tower Suite. Azeem held the door
for her, taking over the loaded cart she was
pushing. With a smile, he invited her inside.
As illogical as it was, she was disappointed.

She didn't want to see Madani, but she did, if only to discern how he was doing.

"The kitchen is right this way," Azeem said.

On the way from the foyer they passed the dining room. The table had already been set with lovely gold-edged china and crystal water goblets. The wine and cocktail glasses were arranged on a tray on the sideboard.

"If there is something you need, you have only to ask," Azeem assured her when they entered the kitchen.

She glanced around. "Everything looks to be in order."

More than in order. The room was as large as her kitchen and nearly as well equipped, she thought, noting the brand name on the appliances. For a man who only visited Manhattan on business a handful of times each year, and who didn't know how to boil water, Madani enjoyed excellent accommodations. Indeed, his were better than the vast majority of native New Yorkers. His export business must be truly thriving.

She began unloading the cart and got down to business. An hour later, as she checked on the sea bass, Madani's guests began arriving.

Emily could hear snippets of their conversations coming from the other room along with Babs Henderson's unmistakable laughter. She wished Madani would come by and put an end to her nervousness. Until she saw him, spoke to him, she was going to worry how their first encounter after almost having sex was going to make her feel.

Her luck, he picked the worst time to walk into the kitchen. She was in the middle of dishing up the hummus dip. She looked up, saw his handsome face and her hands faltered. The next thing she knew a large spoonful of it wound up in the freshly baked pita chips instead of the serving bowl.

"Sorry about that."

"No. I should apologize for startling you."

"It's not your fault."

"I must insist that it is," he replied.

How ridiculous. They were arguing over who was to blame. Some of her awkwardness ebbed away. "Fine. It's all on you, Madani. For shame."

He smiled briefly before sobering. "I was worried you would not come today."

Though Emily had very seriously considered leaving him in the lurch or perhaps swapping places with Arlene, she asked casually, "Why wouldn't I come?"

"We didn't part on the best of terms last night."

"Actually I think we did. It was for the best that things ended before… before they could continue." Heat flared in her face.

She didn't care for the fact that he nodded instead of arguing. "Still, I was worried that I had—how would you say?—crossed the line."

She recalled the way she'd divested him of his shirt and held up her arms so he could pull hers over her head. Fairness demanded she say, "I think we crossed it together."

Madani smiled, albeit sadly. His tone, his words held an uncomfortable amount of finiteness when he told her, "It's a memory I shall cherish. Emily, I have something I need to—"

Before he could finish, the kitchen door swung open and a middle-aged woman entered. She was dressed in a dove-gray uniform and a pair of thick-soled white shoes.

"Good evening, sir," she said to Madani.

"Oh, Emily, this is Mrs. Patterson, my

housekeeper. She will be serving dinner this evening and helping you with anything you require in the kitchen."

"Mrs. Patterson." Emily nodded.

"Well, I should go. You have work to do and my guests are arriving."

"I'll have Mrs. Patterson bring out the hummus dish and pita wedges. That will give your guests something to snack on before they have to take a seat in the dining room. The penne pasta first course is ready as soon as you are."

He nodded and left and, even as her heart took a tumble, Emily got down to business.

Twenty minutes later, Mrs. Patterson returned to the kitchen after serving drinks and appetizers. She cleared her throat. "Excuse me, Emily. Your presence is requested in the dining room."

Although it wasn't unheard of to be summoned from the kitchen during a dinner party, being summoned during this one had her heart hammering. She tucked any hair that had escaped the net back beneath it, smoothed down her chef's coat and, after taking a deep breath, walked out.

"Good evening." She glanced around the table. The Hendersons were there. Another couple looked familiar, too, although she couldn't recall their names. "I trust everything is all right?"

"Fine. Exceptional, as a matter of fact. But…"

Her heart skipped a beat. "But?"

"We would like for you to join us."

"For dinner?" She blinked in surprise. She hadn't seen this coming.

"Please," Babs said. "You know how I am about odd numbers. Our host has agreed to humor me."

"What about your social secretary?"

"If Stella were free this evening I'd call her and make her come. But she has a prior engagement. Besides, you are such an interesting conversationalist, Emily."

She glanced at Madani. His neutral expression gave no clue as to his feelings about the invitation.

"Azeem?" she said hopefully. At least the driver was wearing a suit.

He shook his head. "Apparently the car needs to be washed and waxed."

At this time of night? Sure it did.

"Come on, Emily. The housekeeper can bring another place setting. I'll even move down and give you the chair next to our host."

Babs and her damned quirks. Emily could have killed the socialite. She settled for pointing out the obvious without going into too much detail.

"I'm working tonight, Babs." Not to mention that she still felt awkward around Madani. And then there was the not so small matter of her appearance. Her hair was pulled back and tucked under a requisite net and she was outfitted in a uniform while the other guests wore designer-label evening apparel.

"You can pop in and out as need be while the remaining courses are served," Babs said generously. "We'll all understand."

Emily divided a glance between Madani and the socialite. "It's very kind of you to want to include me, but I'm sure Mr. Tarim is only being polite. I'm his *caterer*."

His brows rose at the emphasis, as if to remind her that being in his employ had not kept her from nearly winding up horizontal with him the night before.

"It was not mere politeness on my part. I wish for you to join us, Emily," he said.

Put that way, how could she refuse?

She took her time plating the sea bass, hoping to get control of her emotions. She could do this without making a fool of herself.

While Mrs. Patterson served the entrée, Emily dashed to the powder room just off the kitchen. There was no help for her attire, but she removed the net and unpinned her hair. Despite a vigorous finger-combing, it remained crimped in some places and flat in others. Well, it would have to do.

When she returned to the dining room, Babs had moved to make room for her. Emily took the seat next to Madani, laying a cloth napkin across the lap of cotton work pants. *Fool,* she thought. And that was before Babs unintentionally tossed out a verbal grenade.

"The sea bass is delightful, Emily." She glanced around the table. "Denby and I are so proud of her and all she has accomplished.

We practically discovered her and here she is five years later, making a meal for a sheikh."

Emily's polite smile dimmed in confusion. "A sheikh?"

"Sheikh Madani Abdul Tarim." Babs frowned. "He didn't allow me to formally introduce him that day in my kitchen, but I assumed you knew."

Emily's ears had begun to buzz. She turned to Madani, feeling oddly betrayed. "You're a sheikh. You told me you were the owner of an export business."

"I am. Among other things."

"You might have mentioned those other things included being the ruler of a country."

"I am not the ruler." He cleared his throat and a dull flush stained his cheeks before he added, "Yet."

"Uh-oh," Babs said sotto voce. "It looks like I may have opened up a can of worms."

Emily reached for her water glass. "No can of worms. I was mistaken about what he did for a living. That's all. But it doesn't matter. I'm only the caterer. It's not like the sheikh owed me the truth."

"Oh. Well, it's a good thing you feel that way," Babs said. Lowering her voice, as if that made any difference when other diners could still hear her, she said, "For a moment, it almost sounded like maybe the two of you were...involved."

"We're not involved," Emily said.

"No," Madani agreed.

"Of course you're not," Babs said with a vigorous nod. "How could you be when Madani is engaged to be married?"

Engaged!

To think a moment ago Emily had been flummoxed to discover he was a sheikh. Her throat worked spasmodically now. It was a good thing she'd already swallowed the sip of water she'd taken. She camouflaged her reaction by dabbing her mouth with her napkin. Too bad the square of fabric wasn't bigger so she could hide behind it and give in to the tears that were stinging her eyes.

"Emily—" Madani began. Beneath the table, his fingers brushed her thigh.

But she turned to Babs. "Yes, he's engaged. And me, well, you know me, Babs. My career is my life."

How she got through the rest of the meal she didn't know. But she did and with a surprising amount of dignity. She even contributed to the conversation, offering her two-cents on global trade. All the while she politely ignored Madani and the hand he periodically rested on her thigh. Dessert was served to rave reviews. Afterward, she excused herself. Her work here was done.

She was packing up her supplies when he entered the kitchen.

"Emily, I owe you…"

She rattled off a dollar amount. At his frown, she clarified, "What you owe me. The truffles cost more than I anticipated."

"I don't care about the money." He was every inch the wealthy ruler when he waved a hand in dismissal of the sum. "I want to apologize."

"For lying to me?" she asked. "Or for cheating on your fiancée?"

"I didn't lie. Nor did I cheat."

"You're engaged!"

"No." Emily's heart lifted, only to plunge again when he added, "Not yet."

"Please don't tell me you think that makes

me feel any better," she whispered. "I was…
and you…we nearly…"

"I know." He heaved a sigh. "I can only
imagine what you must think of me, but I did
not mean for any of this to happen."

Okay, did he think *that* was going to make
her feel better?

She crossed her arms. "Coming by my
apartment last night, staying even after my
assistants left, that wasn't an accident,
Madani. Or Sheikh Tarim." Her hands fell to
her sides. "What do I call you now?"

"I am the same man, Emily. Sheikh is
only a title."

"No. I don't know you." She exhaled
wearily. "I don't know myself. But at least
I'm not in a serious relationship with
someone else and trying to pick up a little on
the side." Her eyes began to sting. "When
were you going to mention her? Or were you
going to at all? And here I thought you were
so different from Reed."

Madani's heart already felt pulverized, but
Emily's mention of her philandering ex-boyfriend delivered a punishing blow. It didn't
matter that he hadn't set out to hurt or
deceive her, he was guilty of both.

"After what happened yesterday…I was going to tell you everything tonight."

"Well, Babs saved you the trouble."

"I mean before the dinner party." He'd paced his bedroom, knowing Emily was in the kitchen and that he owed her the truth. He'd tried to come up with the right words to explain not only his situation, but what she had come to mean to him. But English eluded him despite his longtime fluency. He'd actually had to write out his apology, first in Arabic and then translate it. Finally he'd gone to see her. "But Mrs. Patterson interrupted me and my guests were arriving."

"Your guests." Her face bleached of color. "Go out and see to them. You're the host."

"You are more important to me," he insisted.

"No." Her eyes turned bright. "Please, if you care about me at all, for the sake of my personal and professional reputations, go out there before they begin to talk. As it is, they have reason enough to speculate on the exact nature of our relationship."

He nodded. He would do as she asked.

He'd caused her enough distress. "Promise me you will not leave before we can talk."

"What is there left to say?"

"Promise me." His thoughts turned to the real estate deal he'd struck on Emily's behalf that morning. It had cost him a bundle, but it did little to repay the debt he owed her. "I have something for you."

It was almost an hour before his guests left and Madani could return to the kitchen. Emily was sitting at the table drinking a glass of water.

"Thank you for waiting."

She shrugged. "I said I would."

"I have something for you." He pulled some papers from the inside pocket of his suit coat. "It's my way of saying I'm sorry."

She unfolded the document, a legal agreement for the purchase of the building whose location she'd said was perfect for her restaurant. As he watched, her confusion gave way to comprehension. He waited for a smile, expected some joy. What he got was white-hot fury.

"What is this?" she demanded.

"It's a purchase agreement." He frowned. "I bought the entire building."

"And, what, you're just *giving* it to me?"

"Yes. I want you to have it. You deserve it."

It became apparent immediately that was the wrong thing to say. "Because we nearly slept together? Gee, would I get a small country if we'd actually had sex? Is this your idea of payment for services rendered?"

Madani's eyes widened. He hadn't considered that Emily might view his gift in such an ominous light. "No. Don't think of it like that. My intention was only to make you happy, and to atone for my behavior last night."

She crumpled the papers, tossed them aside. "You lied to me, Madani. You have a fiancée!" Before he could argue, she said, "Excuse me, I forgot. You're not actually engaged yet. But that's semantics in my book. If you love her enough to consider proposing, you should love her enough to be faithful."

"I do not love her! I love…I love…" He released an oath in his native tongue. "You make this so difficult."

She said nothing, though her eyes had

grown wide. Under her watchful gaze, he paced the length of his kitchen. The truth. He needed to reveal the last damning bit, that part that he'd hidden even from himself. Maybe then some of this pain would go away. He stilled, faced her.

"I love *you*, Emily.

"You love… No!" She shook her head and his heart ached anew.

"As preposterous as it may seem, I think I started falling for you the moment Babs introduced us." Had that really been a couple of weeks ago?

"What about your fiancée or girlfriend or whatever? Did you just fall out of love with her?"

"I never fell in. In truth, I barely know her." He walked to the table and smoothed out the documents. "It is an arrangement, not much different than the purchase of this building. It was brokered by our parents when I was but a boy."

"An arranged marriage?" She appeared skeptical. He needed to believe she also was relieved to hear that he didn't love Nawar.

"Yes. They still have those in my country.

They are falling out of fashion and favor, especially among the younger generation, but…" Madani lifted his shoulders.

"Are they…legally binding?"

"Not according to the laws of Kashaqra, but morally…" He thought of his father, again saw Adil slump to the floor. In this case, Madani's future was etched in stone. "I am obligated."

"So you will go through with it."

Jaw clenched, he nodded.

"I see."

No, she didn't. He needed to make her understand. Madani took the seat next to hers and reached for her hand. "You say that I lied to you, Emily. Yes, I did. I lied to myself, too. I thought I could be satisfied to merely spend time with you, to be your friend. But the longer I knew you… You fascinate me on every level. I have never met your equal."

He watched her swallow before she said, "You claim to love me, yet in the same breath you spell out what the future holds for us, or rather, for you." Her voice grew hoarse. Her eyes were bright with tears. "What do you expect me to say to that?"

"I do not know." He'd never felt so power-less, so hopeless and lost. "Perhaps there is nothing for you to say."

Yet he waited, masochist that he was, hoping she would return the sentiment.

Emily pulled her hand from his and stood. "An apology is all I'm due. I accept yours. But I can't accept this." She nodded toward the papers. "It's…too much."

To his mind, it was not nearly enough. Given the chance, he'd give her the world.

"Please," he urged, rising to his feet. "I want you to have it. Opening The Merit is your dream. Let me help you make it come true."

"No."

Her dream?

Emily pondered that as she drove home. Was owning a restaurant *all* she wanted in life? She'd thought so. She'd been quite certain, in fact. Until Madani told her he loved her.

Part of her had thrilled at his declaration. God knew, it had taken restraint she hadn't been aware she possessed to keep her true feelings from spilling out. A glance at the big picture had made it easier to hold them in. He wasn't free. Sheikh or no sheikh, his destiny had been decided long before they'd met, and Emily wasn't part of it.

He'd offered her the building for her restaurant as a consolation prize—one heck of a consolation prize, but a consolation prize nonetheless. Here was her dream on a silver platter. The problem? It wasn't her only dream any longer.

CHAPTER ELEVEN

WHEN Madani answered the phone early the next morning after a sleepless night, it was his mother, and her tone warned him that she was not happy.

"I have called four times in half as many days. Unless you have been stricken too ill to dial a telephone, I will expect both an explanation and an apology."

"I have no excuse, Mother, so I can only apologize. I'm sorry if I worried you."

"As your mother, I expect to worry. It comes with the territory."

"Well, then, I hope your mind is now at ease."

"It would be, but you sound unhappy."

Leave it to Fadilah to decipher his emotions from the opposite side of the planet.

"I am not unhappy," he lied, and poured more coffee from a brass *cezve*. "Preoccupied would be a better word choice."

"*Hmm*. Nawar is preoccupied as well," Fadilah replied, misconstruing his meaning. "Or so her mother tells me. Have you spoken with her?"

He chose to act obtuse. "With Nawar's mother?"

"Not with Bahira," she chided. "Nawar."

Madani could count the number of times he and his betrothed had spoken over the years, either in person or on the telephone. None of their communications had been spontaneous or terribly personal. And none had occurred in recent weeks.

"No. But I trust she is well."

"Yes. I met with her and Bahira for lunch the other day to discuss the menu for the feast. We want it to be extra special given its significance this year. That is the reason for my call."

He sipped his coffee, barely listening. The mention of menus had him thinking of Emily. "I'm sure whatever the three of you decide will be fine."

"Normally I would feel the same way, but Nawar has made an interesting suggestion."

The comment snagged his attention. "Regarding?"

"She said as a way to pay homage to Kashaqra's growing recognition abroad—thanks in part to your efforts to promote our artisans and craftsmen—the menu of the final feast should be international with a sampling of foods from around the globe."

Food…now Emily was definitely on his mind and, though he knew it was pure folly, an idea began to germinate.

"How does Bahira feel about Nawar's suggestion?" he asked diplomatically.

"Bah!" Fadilah spat. "Bahira is too narrow-minded. If it were up to her Kashaqra's borders would be lined with barbed wire fences to prevent outside visitors, and television and the Internet would be banned because of their corrupt influences. She does not welcome simple change much less that which breaks from tradition."

"And you, Mother?"

"I believe in honoring the traditions that have been handed down through the centuries. In doing so, we honor our ancestors.

But I like Nawar's idea for the final feast. Besides, the calendar year contains three hundred and sixty-four other days during which our people can dine on what is familiar." He pictured his mother's mouth turning down as she shrugged.

"So, am I to cast the deciding vote?" he asked.

"You give yourself too much credit," Fadilah chided. "I've already had my head together with the palace chef about the menu."

Madani swallowed. His mother adored the portly Riyad's preparation of regional dishes, but having eaten at some of the finest restaurants abroad, Madani was well aware of the chef's failings when it came to other types of cuisine.

"It's nice to be needed," he inserted dryly. "So why was it necessary to reach me?"

"Nawar thought you might have some favorite dishes that we could include."

He thought of the sea bass and the caramel trifle he'd dined on just the night before. "I do, but Riyad is not experienced enough to do them justice."

"He can learn."

"Or perhaps he can be taught." Foolish or not, the idea grew. He gave it voice. "There is a chef here with whom I've become acquainted that I may be able to persuade to help with the feast. This chef is very skilled with a variety of cuisines."

"Riyad won't like it…" his mother began. Then, "Oh, very well. If we are to serve your favorite dishes it makes sense to have them cooked to your liking. Hire whomever you wish."

After the call ended, Madani scrubbed a hand over his face. What he was thinking was absurd, insane. Assuming Emily agreed with his plan, and that was far from a given, he would be putting himself in the excruciating position of being with her without *being* with her.

Perhaps it was just as well that she hadn't said she loved him, too. That would make it all the more difficult to subjugate his feelings and mask his emotions around his family. But his pain would be worth it if Emily agreed to earn from him what she'd refused to accept as a gift.

* * *

Emily was meeting Donna for drinks, hoping to repair their damaged friendship. She locked the door's dead bolt and tucked her keys in her purse. When she turned to leave, she nearly ran into Madani's chest.

"Hello, Emily."

God, he looked good. She wanted to wrap her arms around him, confess her true feelings and beg him to find a way out of his arranged marriage. For that matter, she wanted to slug him a good one for being so seemingly perfect that she fell for him.

Instead, after silently cursing fate, she steadied her rioting emotions, rallied her pride and said with forced indifference, "I'm just on my way out."

He nodded. "I should have called."

They both knew why he hadn't. She wouldn't have agreed to see him.

"Well, I need to be going. Whatever you came to say will have to wait for another time." Such as the next millennium.

Emily started toward the elevator. When he fell into step beside her, she opted to take the stairs instead. No way was she going to tempt her pathetically weak resolve by spending even a short ride to the lobby in a confined space with him.

"It can't wait, Emily. I must leave soon."

"Oh, that's right. Back to Kashaqra and your almost bride-to-be." The accusation echoed in the stairwell.

"Yes," he agreed flatly.

Emily gritted her teeth. So *now* he was all for being open and honest. "I fail to see what that has to do with me."

"I assume you have not changed your mind about accepting the building."

"No."

"Then I have a business proposition to make."

That stopped her. She turned and stared at him. "I don't understand?"

"Each summer in my country, we celebrate the Feast of Seven Days to mark the long-ago ouster of a repressive ruler who all but starved to death many of the Kashaqran people. In the capital city, the feast is very elaborate and everyone is given time off from work to join in."

It sounded exciting and exotic, two things

Emily's life wasn't…or hadn't been, until she'd met Madani.

He was saying, "As is the tradition, members of my family oversee all of the capital city's preparations, including the menu."

Despite her better judgment, her curiosity was piqued. "Menu?"

"This year will include delicacies from all over the globe." Just as her epicurean juices began to flow, he added, "At the final feast, my betrothal to Nawar will be announced."

Her interest soured. "So, it's going to be an engagement party and the whole country's invited to help you celebrate."

She started down the stairs.

"Unfortunately the palace chef is not what I would call competent when it comes to cooking other kinds of cuisine," he said, again in step beside her.

"I see your dilemma." Emily picked up her pace.

"I would like to hire you to assemble the menu and then assist the chef and kitchen staff in the preparations."

She couldn't have heard him correctly,

which was why she stopped a second time and gaped at him.

"I am asking a lot. I know."

A lot? Try too much. Last night he'd said he loved her. Today, all he apparently loved was her cooking. And she'd thought her heart was done breaking.

She lifted her chin. "I'm sorry, Sheikh. It sounds like a wonderful opportunity, but I'm going to have to pass. I don't do big events. Too assembly-line for my taste, remember?"

"I remember. Believe me, Emily. Nothing that occurred during our time together will ever escape my memory."

Why did he have to say something like that? Why did the same have to be true for her?

"If you say yes, you will be generously compensated," Madani said after a moment. He pulled a sheaf of papers from his pocket.

Figuring she knew what they were, Emily gritted her teeth in indignation and let anger take the lead. "I thought I made it clear that I cannot and will not accept that."

"As a gift." He nodded. "But what about as payment for your time and talent?"

"I'm no expert on Manhattan real estate, but that building has to be worth millions of dollars."

"Yes, my original offer was too much. I realize that, which is why I have decided to retain ownership of the building. In return for your catering services, I will allow you to use the square footage at street level for the next three years rent-free."

"No."

"Two years, but no less. You would be— what do they say?—selling yourself short."

Emily shook her head, but Madani didn't relent.

"At least take a few days to think about it before giving me your final answer."

"It's not going to change."

"A few days," he repeated. "Please."

"Why?" she demanded. "Why are you doing this to me, to yourself?" She hated that the words wobbled.

"I want you to have your dream, Emily." He'd said the same thing the evening before.

How ironic that the man she'd been in a long-term relationship with hadn't been supportive at all on this matter, while the man with whom she could have no future, stood fully behind her.

"Dreams change," she murmured. At Madani's frown, she said briskly, "I can make The Merit a reality without you. The only difference is the timeline."

"You don't need me." She heard pride in his tone even as his gaze turned sad. "Your independence and determination are just two of the qualities I've come to admire. You are also an astute businesswoman. What I am asking you to consider is a business arrangement."

They reached the lobby and he held the door for her. As she passed by, he brushed his knuckles lightly over her cheek. In a voice ripe with anguish he said, "You will never know how deeply I wish I had more to offer you."

"So a sheikh says he wishes he could offer you more." Donna sipped her apple martini and sighed. "You've really come up in the world since Reed Benedict."

After some initial restraint and awkwardness, the two friends had apologized, hugged,

cried and then fallen back into the easy cama-
raderie that had long marked their relationship. Two martinis later, Emily had opened
up about Madani. She'd told her old friend
everything, including the heated interlude in
her kitchen, Madani's declaration of love last
evening and what had transpired just an hour
before on her apartment's stairwell.

"Just a wealthier version of the same."

"You think so?"

"You don't?"

Donna shook her head. "First of all, he urged
you to reconcile with me. That makes him a
saint in my book. Reed must have been pleased
as punch when the two of us stopped
speaking."

"He didn't like you," Emily agreed diplomatically.

"He hated my guts and it was mutual."
Donna lifted her shoulders dismissively before
going on. "Unlike Reed, your sheikh believes
in your talent, so much so that he bought you
a damned building for your restaurant."

"He's not my sheikh."

Donna ignored her and sighed again.
"Why can't I meet a man like that?"

"He's also the closest thing there is to engaged, yet he never mentioned it. Remember?" Emily reached for her drink.

"That was wrong of him, I'll admit. He should have been up-front. But in his defense, it *is* an arranged marriage. It's you he loves."

Warmth trickled through Emily. She blamed it on the gin in her martini. "He's going to wed someone else."

Donna's expression turned sympathetic. "I'm sorry, Em. But look on the bright side. At least he's not marrying your sister."

"There is that." Emily set her drink aside and lowered her head into her hands. "Oh, Donna. What was I thinking? I shouldn't have gotten involved with him in any way except professionally. My schedule is too hectic."

"So? You can't let what Reed did dictate your views on men and relationships. Reed was the wrong guy for you. When the right one comes along, everything will work out because both of you will be willing to make any necessary sacrifices to see that it does." Donna took a deep breath before going on.

"At the risk of jeopardizing our friendship again with my big mouth, I think you should call your sheikh and accept his business offer."

"He's not *my* sheikh." Emily raised her head. "He's *nothing* to me. He can't be."

"Then you should have no problem working for him again," Donna replied lightly. More seriously she added, "Look, Em, a million other caterers would kill for an opportunity to put something like this on their résumés. Imagine the cache it will give you not only as a caterer, but when you open your restaurant. Emily Merit, chef to the sheikh."

"Have you forgotten I would basically be catering his engagement party?"

"I didn't say it would be easy. But you know how in the old Westerns when a cowboy gets bit by a rattler he cuts the spot open to suck the venom from the wound?"

"You think it would help me get over him."

"Couldn't hurt." Donna shrugged. "Besides, you've dreamed of opening your own restaurant forever. He's putting the opportunity within reach right now. Separate the professional from the personal, Em. This is the chance of a lifetime."

"I don't know." But God help her, she was wavering.

Donna grinned. "And then there's the real bonus. It will take you out of the country on the day your sister gets married."

Emily told herself that was the capper: professional fulfillment *and* an airtight excuse for skipping Elle's nuptials. It had nothing to do with the fact that she was eager to see Madani's homeland and experience firsthand his culture, even if only so she could let him go.

After reaching her decision, she waited two days to tell him. She caught him the morning he was to leave for Kashaqra.

"I've decided to accept your offer," she said as soon as he came on the line. "I'll come to your country, help with the menu preparations for your…your feast."

"Emily, I—"

She talked over him. "This is an excellent business opportunity. A friend of mine helped me to see that. As she said, in addition to the other compensation you have offered, helping with the feast will give my professional reputation a substantial boost. As such, it's an offer too good to refuse."

Her words were greeted with protracted silence. Finally, he replied, "I am glad you are able to see it that way."

"I do have one request, though."

"Yes?"

"I wish to leave before the big announcement."

There was only so much venom she was willing to suck.

During the month between the time Madani returned to Kashaqra and she was to arrive for the feast preparations, Emily compiled dish selections, which she e-mailed to him. Each time she received the same reply: *Many thanks. I look forward to your arrival.—M*

Did he? Or was he just being polite?

She didn't take time to ponder it. She was too busy. Exhaustingly so. In addition to her hectic catering schedule—which had picked up as word of her cooking for a sheikh spread, courtesy of Babs—Emily spent her mornings with a contractor at the building that was to house The Merit. She'd loved it from the outside, had known immediately that the location was prime. The inside, however, needed work and a lot of it to make it conform to her vision.

Already a couple of walls had been moved to accommodate more seating in what was to become the dining room, and the site of the new kitchen was set to be renovated. The work would wipe out her savings, but Emily felt confident that with no lease to pay for two years, her bank would approve a loan to cover kitchen appliances and start-up costs.

She was excited about the restaurant. How could she not be? Still, she'd expected to feel a greater sense of fulfillment and satisfaction. Instead, what she felt at times was empty. It didn't help that Madani was always on her mind.

Her cell phone trilled as she paced through sawdust at The Merit. She grimaced upon answering since it was her sister.

"Emily, I'm at the bridal salon and I need to know this very minute if you are going to stand up in my wedding. Final alterations have to be made no later than next week and the dress is going to have to be let out if Constance is to wear it," Elle complained.

Emily rubbed her eyes wearily. "I've told you time and again I'm not standing up in your wedding. I won't be there, period. I'll be out of the country on a job."

Her mother wasn't happy about it. Her father had even stopped by the apartment to lecture Emily on her obligations to the family. She'd held firm despite the guilt and pressure. Elle, as self-serving as ever, made it easier.

"Oh, that's right. You'd rather go to Kenya and play chef for that sheikh guy."

"Kashaqra. It's one continent over."

Elle snorted. "Whatever. Geometry was never my strong suit." Emily decided to let that one slide.

"God, you are such a hypocrite!" Elle shouted.

"Excuse me."

"You're still upset about Reed seeing me behind your back, yet the guy you were all over at my shower cheats with you and you're all forgive and forget."

Emily's stomach knotted. "What do you mean?"

"I told you his name sounded familiar. That's because he was featured in *Chatter* a couple of months ago. I found the magazine in my nightstand this morning and reread it. Imagine my surprise upon discovering your boyfriend topped the list of the World's Hunkiest Billionaires. I was happy for you until I got to the part about him being taken. Apparently you have no problem being the other woman."

"I didn't know about his…status," she said slowly.

"You would have if you read something other than recipe books."

"Well, I don't."

"You do now," Elle said pointedly.

"I'm going to Kashaqra on business."

But she knew she was lying. She was going to Kashaqra to say goodbye.

CHAPTER TWELVE

"WHAT are you thinking?" Azeem shouted the question as he marched into the office.

Madani glanced up in surprise. "Excuse me?"

"The person you've asked me to collect from the airport is Emily Merit. She is the American chef hired to help with the feast preparations."

Azeem's face turned a deeper shade of red and he let out a string of expletives.

Madani rose to his feet, confused by his friend's rage. "What is your objection? Emily is very good at what she does."

"She must be, for she has you thinking with something other than your head," Azeem shot back.

Madani was grateful for the expanse of

desk that separated them, because the insulting comment made him angry enough to want to take a swing.

"Take care with your words," he warned. "You go too far."

"No. It is *you* who goes too far." Azeem's thick hands fisted at his sides, proof of his own restraint. "You are bringing your mistress here, flaunting her in Nawar's face just days before the betrothal announcement. I know you do not love Nawar, that your marriage to her is but the result of a bargain struck to bolster family alliances. But this…this is an outrage! I will not stand for it."

Some of Madani's fury ebbed into confusion over Azeem's vehement defense of Nawar's honor. He decided to stir things up in the hope of eventually making them clearer. "I believe you were the one who suggested I have a fling while in Manhattan. You even chided me for leaving Emily's apartment that one evening and offered to take me back."

"Yes, but that was when—" Azeem's mouth snapped closed and he glanced away.

"When what?"

"Nothing."

"Don't hold back now, *sadiqi*," Madani drawled.

"When I thought there was still a chance you might not go through with the wedding. You seemed drawn to Emily. We hoped…"

"We?"

Azeem closed his eyes and said nothing. His defeated posture spoke volumes. Understanding dawned. Madani wondered why he hadn't realized it before. "You love Nawar."

His friend didn't deny it. When his gaze returned to Madani, it was filled with devastation, but nonetheless direct. "If you are going to marry her, you will honor her. You will treat her with respect. I will not stand by and watch her humiliated either in private or before the entire country."

"Emily is not my mistress. I give you my word that is not why I made arrangements to bring her to Kashaqra."

"Then why?"

"I wished only to give her an opportunity, one she richly deserves but would not accept outright." Madani explained briefly about her restaurant plans and the real estate deal. He sighed then. "Foolishly, perhaps selfishly, I am eager to see her one last time and know that she was once in Kashaqra."

Azeem studied him a moment. "You are in love with her."

"I am." He expected his friend to start in again on finding a way out of the marital arrangement. Instead, Azeem dropped heavily into the chair on the opposite side of the desk.

"How is it possible, *sadiqi*, that we have both fallen in love with women we cannot have?"

Later that afternoon, when Azeem went to the airport to meet Emily's plane, Madani didn't go with him. He wanted to welcome her to his homeland, perhaps take her on a tour of the capital city, but the encounter with Azeem made it clear he couldn't risk the spread of rumors. Neither Emily nor Nawar deserved to be put in such an unflattering light and forced to fend off the resulting gossip and character attacks.

That didn't keep him from pacing his rooms in the palace waiting for word from Azeem that she had arrived safely.

Emily felt as if she'd been whisked into a fairy tale. She'd felt that way since the plane touched down at Kashaqra's largest airport. She'd expected, foolishly hoped, that Madani would be there to greet her. But it was his driver who stood at the gate perusing the faces of deplaning passengers.

"Hello, Emily. I trust your flight was uneventful," Azeem inquired politely when she reached him.

"Yes." She'd experienced a lot of turbulence, all of it internal.

She forgot about it as the car, a Mercedes similar to the one he'd driven in Manhattan, left the airport and headed to the palace. She'd scoured the Internet for information and images of Kashaqra. None of it prepared her for the reality. The countryside was surprisingly homey and while not lush due to the arid conditions, nothing about it was barren. It was sprinkled with humble homes and farms.

In the distance, mountains rose up, stretching majestically on the horizon. Long before the car reached them, Emily would arrive in the capital city. Already she could make out a modern skyline. The closer the buildings drew, the more intrigued she became about the place Madani called home. Seeing it answered some of her questions, and created others. He was to rule one day. Was it what he wanted? Or, like his marriage, was it another aspect of his destiny that others had determined?

When they reached the city limits, the rooflines along the well-tended streets grew taller and more elaborate. She'd grown up in New York, taking feats of engineering for granted. She let her head fall back now and gazed through the sunroof at buildings that, while not quite as tall as what could be found back home, were every bit as amazing.

"This city has some incredible architecture," she murmured.

"It does."

She lowered her gaze, noting the sidewalks where vendors were hawking their goods and people sat outside at cafés eating and sipping beverages. "It's not so different from Manhattan."

She caught Azeem's reflection in the rearview mirror and smiled.

"I believe our city has two million fewer residents than yours does, but yes, it's similar. I think that is why Madani feels so at home in both places."

A dozen questions bubbled to mind—not about the country, but about the man. She bit them back and listened instead as Azeem noted some sites of interest. The last one he pointed out, however, left them both frowning.

"Down that street is the large park where much of the festivities will be held, including the food tents." More quietly, he added, "It also is where Madani's parents will announce his betrothal on the final night."

This time, Emily wasn't able to suppress the question that most weighed on her mind. "Is he happy, Azeem?"

"Are you happy?"

Emily blinked, as surprised by his question as the knowing look in his eyes.

"What reason would I have to be otherwise?"

"The same reason as Madani perhaps?"

When they arrived at the palace a few minutes later, Emily's nerves were jangling. The time was at hand. But when she entered a grand hall with mosaic tiled floors and arched ceilings, Madani wasn't there to greet her. Emily chided herself for thinking he would be. A sheikh, one whose engagement was soon to be announced, surely had better things to do with his time than meet the hired help.

"If you will come this way." Azeem led her down a corridor to a cozier room set up with comfortable chairs and sofas that were upholstered in rich hues. Three women were inside. Was it Emily's imagination, or did the young one smile sadly at Azeem?

One of the older women stretched out her hand in the standard Western greeting and confirmed Emily's worst nightmare when she said in perfect English, "I am Fadilah Tarim, Madani's mother. Welcome to Kashaqra, Miss Merit."

"Thank you." Should she bow, curtsy,

genuflect? Even as Emily contemplated proper protocol, Madani's mother was introducing the others.

"This is Nawar, my son's bride-to-be. And Nawar's mother, Bahira."

All of them were lovely and fashionably attired. Emily felt frumpy in her wrinkled rose blouse and camel trousers. For one terrifying moment, Emily wondered if she was going to be ill, but she managed to hold down the contents of her stomach and offered a weak smile. "It's a pleasure to meet all of you and may I offer my congratulations?"

She thanked her lucky stars they also spoke English since her grasp of Arabic was severely limited.

"Thank you." Nawar nodded. Her smile was sweet, but again seemed sad. "Of course, it is not official yet."

"It will be soon enough." This from Bahira.

Nawar's complexion paled. Apparently Emily wasn't the only one suffering from nausea.

"Our chef has prepared several of the recipes you sent in advance of your arrival.

My son is critical of his results. He says you are a much better cook."

"That's too kind."

"We are pleased you could come and lend your expertise to this year's feast," Fadilah said.

"Yes, especially given its added significance." Bahira eyed Emily with unabashed speculation, before saying something rather heated in Arabic.

Madani's mother flushed, whether out of embarrassment or anger, Emily wasn't sure. She smiled tightly. "You must excuse my friend. In her excitement she has forgotten to use English."

Bahira was undeterred. "I said I am surprised to find that the chef Madani insisted on is so young and attractive."

It was Emily's face that heated this time. "I am highly regarded in New York. If references would put you at ease about my qualifications, I will gladly supply them."

"That will not be necessary," Fadilah inserted with finality. To the other matron she said, "Young women, attractive or otherwise, pursue professions and often rise to the top, Bahira. It is unfair to discount Miss Merit's abilities based solely on her appearance."

"You are right, Fadilah." Nawar's mother tipped her head to one side as if in concession, but her gaze remained cold.

"We won't keep you, Miss Merit," Fadilah said. "You must be tired after your long flight. I will ring for a maid to take you to your room. If there is anything you need, simply ask."

The only thing Emily needed was a stiff drink. She'd made a mistake by coming here, a huge one. She'd thought she could be professional, concentrate on the contract between her and Madani and forget about the contract between his family and Nawar's. But as she'd looked into the lovely face of his bride-to-be, all she could think was, Madani loves me.

This was ten times more painful than staying in Manhattan, outfitting herself in peach organdy and watching Reed marry Elle.

Forget her career. Forget closure and sucking out venom. She couldn't do this.

* * *

Madani paced his rooms with the desperation of a caged animal. Emily was under the same roof as he was and as far away as ever. He could not go to her, not even on the pretext of welcoming her to his homeland. A knock interrupted his thoughts. He answered the door to find his mother standing on the other side. One look at her expression and he knew whatever she had to say was not going to be pleasant.

"The American chef you hired is a woman!" she shouted, sweeping into the room with her arms crossed and her eyes flashing. "A young and beautiful woman."

"That makes her no less capable."

Her head jerked in a nod. "The very thing I told Bahira when she commented on it. But I doubt my assurances stopped her concern. Nor will they stop the rumors that are bound to swirl. What possessed you to do this, Madani?"

"She is an excellent chef. Brilliant. You will see when you sample her work. She will put Riyad's cooking to shame. She is beyond compare."

"There is something you are not telling

me," Fadilah accused. Then her tone turned pleading. "Madani, your engagement is to be announced soon. Now is not the time for…for…indiscretions." She waved one delicate hand.

He reached for it, squeezed it. "I am not being indiscreet. That I can promise you."

Fadilah freed her hand from his to lay it against his cheek as she had often done when he was a child. It could not soothe the ache he felt now.

"But you have feelings for this woman that go beyond professional."

"I will marry Nawar as is expected. I will not do anything to upset Father."

She frowned at that. "Your father is fine. His health is far from fragile these days."

"And it will stay that way."

Fadilah turned to leave. She stopped at the door. "This Emily Merit, who is she to you, Madani?"

"She is…" *The woman I want to wake up to after a long night of lovemaking. The woman whose mind I want a chance to change about marriage and children. The woman whom in a very short amount of time*

I have come to love beyond all reason. But he shook his head, denying his desire, denying his heart. "It doesn't matter. She can be no one to me."

CHAPTER THIRTEEN

EMILY found her way to the palace kitchen the following morning. She would leave as soon as it could be arranged. Before then, she would do her best to see that the feast preparations were under way.

She was showing the palace chef her technique for making an apple almond tart's thick crust when Madani's mother entered.

"Riyad." Fadilah smiled at the heavy-set man. "I need to speak to Miss Merit in private. Will you leave us for a moment?"

When he was gone, Emily dusted flour from her hands and waited. It was a moment before Fadilah said, "I have a problem, Miss Merit. It involves my son."

That made two of them. Striving for nonchalance, Emily said, "He is well, I hope?"

"Physically, yes. Emotionally, Madani is…confused." Fadilah fussed with the elaborately embroidered sleeve of her dress, giving her words time to sink in. "All of Kashaqra will soon learn of his betrothal to Nawar. Though the announcement will be made officially, it has been common knowledge among many of our people for years. He may have mentioned to you that the agreement between our families was made when he was a young boy and Nawar a baby."

"He mentioned it."

Fadilah nodded. "He has, most inconveniently, I might add, met someone. I think he believes himself to be in love with this woman. I think perhaps she may even have tender feelings for him."

"I do," she replied honestly. "But you needn't worry. I am not here to try to stop anything."

"Then why did you come?" The question seemed more like a challenge.

Emily didn't want to discuss the feelings that had brought her here, so she only said, "Business. I was hired to help prepare the feast. It's the opportunity of a lifetime."

"Madani mentioned that you run a successful catering company in Manhattan." Fadilah motioned toward the tart crust on which Emily and Riyad had been working. "Having sampled some of your work this past week, I see that my son did not overstate your skill."

"Thank you. I am opening a restaurant, too."

"I would imagine doing so takes a lot of money, especially in Manhattan."

"It does." Emily notched up her chin and said, "That's another reason I'm here."

"But those aren't the only reasons, are they?" Fadilah's gaze was shrewd.

"No. I wanted to see Kashaqra."

Fadilah's brow puckered. "Why?"

"It's…it's Madani's home, part of who he is."

"You wanted to see my son again."

"One last time, yes," Emily admitted around the lump in her throat.

Fadilah studied her for a maddening moment, before saying, "In many ways, Miss Merit, I am a businesswoman, too. My family is my business. And so I have an offer to make you."

"An offer?"

"I will pay you triple the amount you've been promised if you leave Kashaqra in the morning."

Though she'd already planned to leave, Emily's stomach knotted. "I signed a contract with your son."

"Contracts can be broken. Think about it and give me your answer later today."

As she stared at the door through which Fadilah had left, Emily knew contracts weren't the only things that could be broken.

It was madness, but when Madani spied Emily in the courtyard garden later that day, his resolve to stay away from her fled. As she admired the lush blooms on one of his mother's rosebushes, she looked incredibly beautiful and deeply troubled.

"Hello, Emily."

She started at the sound of his voice. "Madani. I wasn't expecting… It's lovely out here."

"My mother's doing. She tends the rosebushes herself."

"Yes, she's very hands-on," Emily murmured.

He wasn't sure what she meant by the comment. In any event, he had no desire to discuss his mother. Work seemed a safe topic, so he asked, "How is the restaurant? Any new developments there?"

"It's funny you should mention that."

When she would have dipped her head, he put his fingers beneath her chin and raised it. "You are happy, yes?"

She had to be happy. Knowing he was helping her dream materialize was the only thing that mitigated the torture he was experiencing having her so close.

"I thought I would be. I should be. The restaurant is what I've wanted, dreamed of. But…"

"But what?"

"It doesn't matter."

"Everything about you matters to me."

She shook her head and pushed to her feet. "No. That's just the sort of thing you can't say. And it's exactly why I must leave."

"Leave?"

"I shouldn't have come to Kashaqra. I thought I could do this."

"Do what?"

"Put on a professional exterior, pretend my heart is not breaking. I can't, because it is. It has been ever since Babs told me you're going to marry someone else."

"Oh, Emily." How was it possible to be miserable and elated at the same time? Madani gave in to the need to touch her and reached for her hand. "I've missed you."

"Don't say that." The demand lacked heat, but she pulled her hand free.

"I only speak the truth."

"Lie to me!" she pleaded. "Don't you get it, Madani? I don't want the truth from you. That only makes it worse. Lie to me. Tell me you don't think about me. Tell me you haven't missed me. Lie," she pleaded a second time.

"Why?"

She shook her head, backed up a step. The answer was there in her eyes, but he needed to hear the words.

He took both of her hands in his this time. "Say it. Just once. Tell me you've fallen in

love with me. Say the words. Please." They
would have to sustain him for a lifetime.

"I love you," she whispered brokenly. He
swore her declaration echoed off the stone
walls.

"Emily." He tugged her into his arms and
whispered her name a second time just
before their mouths met. Need. Madani
ached from it. But before he could lose
himself in the kiss, she was pulling away.

"I can't do this. I…can't," she cried mis-
erably.

When she turned to leave, he let her.

Emily waited until her emotions were under
control before requesting a meeting with
Fadilah. Unfortunately only so much could
be done with her red-rimmed eyes.

"You've accepted my offer," the older
woman deduced. Was it Emily's imagination
or did Fadilah look disappointed?

"Not exactly, but I do wish to return to
Manhattan. Today. Or as soon as possible."

"As soon as possible?" The other woman's
brows rose. "That can be arranged, of course,
but I am curious. When I first broached the

subject, you mentioned that you'd signed a contract with Madani. Does he know that you've changed your mind?"

"I...I think so." Had she told him? Emily wasn't sure. "Will you see to it that he knows?"

Fadilah's disapproval was palpable. "Of course. What reason should I give for your hasty departure? I assume you will not want him to know of our earlier conversation."

"My sister is getting married this weekend. I wasn't planning to attend the ceremony." To think, Emily had once thought attending would be too painful. "We had a falling out."

"But now you have decided to make amends."

"Yes. It will make my parents happy."

Oddly, Fadilah frowned at that.

"I'm packed and I've left Riyad with step-by-step instructions on how to prepare the dishes that were selected for the feast. Everything will work out for the best."

Fadilah's frown deepened. "Perhaps. I will inform Azeem of your plans and have him bring a car around within the hour. Before you leave, I will give you the agreed upon funds."

Emily rose. "Thank you, but that isn't necessary."

"Emily is gone?"

Madani stood in the doorway of his parents' private sitting room. His parents had requested to see him. Of all the topics he'd thought they might want to discuss, Emily was not one.

"She left this evening for the airport. Her flight to Manhattan is probably boarding as we speak," his mother said.

"But the feast starts in a matter of days."

"Riyad will see to it," Adil replied with a shrug.

Fadilah chuckled as she reached for a slice of pear. "He is more than happy to do so since he considered it an insult that you brought in an outsider in the first place."

"But we had a contract," he argued weakly.

"A lucrative one." His mother smiled. "But I offered her more money to leave."

"What!"

"Calm yourself. She didn't take it."

Fadilah waved a hand. "Now, stop hovering in the doorway. Come sit down. We have much to discuss."

Madani hadn't even taken a seat yet when his father announced, "I'm disappointed in you."

He landed heavily on the chair's cushion. "I didn't mean for this to happen."

"But it did and you said not a word. Indeed, you allowed the preparations for your engagement feast to continue, you even invited this young woman here to help with them."

"I wanted to see her and I wanted her to see Kashaqra," he explained, hoping to keep his father's blood pressure low.

"Because you love her," Adil said.

It was Madani's heart that felt ready to give out now. "Yes."

"Yet even now you would marry Nawar." His father's gaze narrowed.

"I...no. I cannot." He split his gaze between his parents, waiting for the fallout, praying his father would remain calm.

Adil remained more than calm. He grinned. "Finally, my son, you are acting like a ruler."

"I don't understand."

"Madani, I held firm on the marriage contract because I believed you would eventually come to love Nawar. She is, after all, a fine young woman and your arguments against the arrangement didn't have anything to do with your heart. They do now."

"Yes."

"You love Emily." Fadilah smiled. "And she loves you, too. Which is why she fled. Will you go after her?"

"But what about the feast? Nawar?"

"I think we can handle them, both. So?" Fadilah's brows rose.

Madani's response was to jump from his seat and bolt for the door.

Emily made it through the wedding ceremony, smiling as instructed during the hour-long photo shoot in the church afterward. Nothing could make her feel worse than she already did and that included wearing the hideous peach organdy dress whose puffy shoulders made her look as if she should be playing offense for the New York Jets.

At the reception, she raised her glass of

champagne in toast to the new Mr. and Mrs. Reed Benedict and choked down the over-cooked food, all while ignoring the pitying looks her aunts and cousins tossed her way.

The only thing that kept her from going insane was Donna's presence. Her friend had insisted on coming with her. They were seated at separate tables for the meal due to Emily's wedding party duties, but once the plates were cleared and the music started, she brought Emily a gin and tonic and hustled her to a secluded corner of the banquet hall. Music pulsed from the huge stereo speakers. But that wasn't why Emily had a headache.

"Hang in there," Donna said. "The bridal dance will be over soon and we can leave."

"Can't wait."

"We can burn your dress in my fireplace. I bet it will go up in a matter of seconds, no lighter fluid necessary."

"Sure." But she was barely listening. What was Madani doing right now? she wondered. What was he feeling? His engagement would become a matter of public record in less than twenty-four hours.

"Hey, Em." Donna elbowed her side.

"There's a guy looking at you. A really good-looking guy."

"Don't mention men to me, good-looking or otherwise. I've sworn off of them. And this time I mean it." She took a liberal swig of her drink and coughed after swallowing. "God, this tastes like straight booze. Did you have them put any tonic in it?"

"He's coming this way. Maybe he wants to ask you to dance."

Emily stirred her drink without looking up. "Not interested."

Donna whistled. "God, I think he could be that underwear model whose picture is plastered all over the city."

Her head snapped up and she scanned the crowd. No. It couldn't be, but then she spied Madani and the breath squeezed from her lungs. She rose on shaky legs, met him halfway across the room. That put them in the center of the dance floor during a fast song. Half a dozen gyrating couples were forced to move around them. She didn't care.

"I can't believe you're here. *Why* are you here?" She had to shout the words to be heard over the music.

"I came for you."

"But your engagement—"

"Has been called off to the relief of nearly everyone involved."

"I don't understand."

The song ended. The dance floor cleared. Murmurs began among the guests. The DJ came on the microphone. "Someone has requested a slow song for the couple now on the dance floor."

Emily glanced up to see Donna standing next to one of the speakers. Her friend raised her glass of gin and tonic and grinned. Madani took Emily's hand. Without the thumping bass, the music didn't seem as loud. Or maybe it was just easier to hear Madani since she was in his arms, her temple pressed to his cheek.

"I think you should know that your mother offered me money to leave the country."

"Yes. It was her way of being sure that you truly love me. It was a lucrative sum, I understand."

His chest rumbled with a laugh, but Emily wanted to be clear on this point, "I didn't take her money."

"Nor would you take anything from me."

"It's only right."

He leaned back, his expression as intense as his tone. "No. It's not right. Your restaurant, Emily—"

"I'll open it someday. Or I won't. Oddly enough, it's no longer the most important thing in my life, though I still plan to do it eventually."

"Maybe you can open a second one in Kashaqra."

She liked the sound of that. "Maybe." She frowned then. "Speaking of contracts, you made it seem as if the arrangement with Nawar's family was set in stone."

"I thought it was. Or, perhaps for the sake of my father's health, I resigned myself to believing that. But after seeing you in the garden, I couldn't lose you. I was determined to find a way around it." The arm around her waist tightened as if he never planned to let her go. "Then I didn't have to. It turns out, my father wants me to marry the woman I love."

"Love." She smiled, felt her heart lift. "It's an impossible emotion to deny."

"It is indeed."

Emily's eyes filled with tears. "You're here. I can't believe you're here."

He stopped dancing and dried her damp cheeks. "Where else would I be, where else *could* I be, when I love you so much?" He turned to the crowd of guests, many of whom were openly gawking. "I love her," he said loudly.

The commotion his announcement caused all but drowned out the music. Elle wasn't going to be happy to be upstaged, especially on her wedding day. None of that mattered right now.

"I love you, too," Emily told him, returning to his arms for a kiss.

When it ended a few minutes later, the sleeves of her peach gown were crumpled a mess, and the spray of flowers that had been in her hair had fallen to the dance floor.

Madani tugged at the collar of his shirt. "Please tell me you don't need to stay."

"I don't." Emily smiled. "What I need— all I need— is you."

MILLS & BOON® ROMANCE

is proud to present

Jewels of the Desert

Deserts, diamonds and destiny!

The Kingdom of Quishari: two rulers, with hearts as
hard as the rugged landscape they reign over,
are in need of Desert Queens…

When they offer convenient proposals, will they
discover doing your duty doesn't have to
mean ignoring your heart?

Sheikh Rashid and his twin brother Sheikh Khalid
are looking for brides in…

ACCIDENTALLY THE SHEIKH'S WIFE

And

MARRYING THE SCARRED SHEIKH

by Barbara McMahon

in April 2010

MILLS & BOON® ROMANCE

is proud to present

THE BRIDES OF BELLA ROSA

Romance, rivalry and a family reunited

Lisa Firenze and Luca Casali's sibling rivalry has torn apart the quiet, sleepy Italian town of Monta Correnti for years…

Now, as the feud is handed down to their children, will history repeat itself? Can the next generation undo their parents' mistakes and reunite their families?

Or are there more secrets to be revealed…?

The saga begins in May 2010 with

BEAUTY AND THE RECLUSIVE PRINCE
by Raye Morgan

and

EXECUTIVE: EXPECTING TINY TWINS
by Barbara Hannay

Don't miss this fabulous sequel to BRIDES OF BELLA LUCIA!

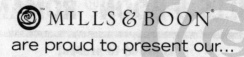

are proud to present our…

Book of the Month

The Major and the Pickpocket
by Lucy Ashford
from Mills & Boon® Historical

Tassie bit her lip. Why hadn't he turned her
over to the constables? She certainly wasn't
going to try to run past him – he towered over
her, six foot of hardened muscle, strong booted
legs set firmly apart. Major Marcus Forrester.
All ready for action. And Tassie couldn't
help but remember his kiss…

Mills & Boon® Historical
Available 5th March

Something to say about our
Book of the Month?
Tell us what you think!
millsandboon.co.uk/community

BRIDES OF BELLA LUCIA

A family torn apart by secrets, reunited by marriage

Two fantastic collections containing four full-length stories each, following the scandalous Valentine family and their exclusive Bella Lucia restaurant empire

FREE ONLINE READ!

Brides of Bella Lucia:
Unexpected Proposals

Available
5th March 2010

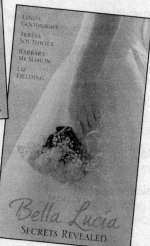

Brides of Bella Lucia:
Secrets Revealed

Available
2nd April 2010

millsandboon.co.uk Community

Join Us!

The Community is the perfect place to meet and chat to kindred spirits who love books and reading as much as you do, but it's also the place to:

- **Get the inside scoop from authors about their latest books**
- **Learn how to write a romance book with advice from our editors**
- **Help us to continue publishing the best in women's fiction**
- **Share your thoughts on the books we publish**
- **Befriend other users**

Forums: Interact with each other as well as authors, editors and a whole host of other users worldwide.

Blogs: Every registered community member has their own blog to tell the world what they're up to and what's on their mind.

Book Challenge: We're aiming to read 5,000 books and have joined forces with The Reading Agency in our inaugural Book Challenge.

Profile Page: Showcase yourself and keep a record of your recent community activity.

Social Networking: We've added buttons at the end of every post to share via digg, Facebook, Google, Yahoo, technorati and de.licio.us.

www.millsandboon.co.uk

2 FREE BOOKS
AND A SURPRISE GIFT

We would like to take this opportunity to thank you for reading this Mills & Boon® book by offering you the chance to take TWO more specially selected books from the Romance series absolutely FREE! We're also making this offer to introduce you to the benefits of the Mills & Boon® Book Club™—

- **FREE home delivery**
- **FREE gifts and competitions**
- **FREE monthly Newsletter**
- **Exclusive Mills & Boon Book Club offers**
- **Books available before they're in the shops**

Accepting these FREE books and gift places you under no obligation to buy, you may cancel at any time, even after receiving your free shipment. Simply complete your details below and return the entire page to the address below. You don't even need a stamp!

YES Please send me 2 free Romance books and a surprise gift. I understand that unless you hear from me, I will receive 5 superb new stories every month including two 2-in-1 books priced at £4.99 each and a single book priced at £3.19, postage and packing free. I am under no obligation to purchase any books and may cancel my subscription at any time. The free books and gift will be mine to keep in any case.

Ms/Mrs/Miss/Mr_____ Initials _____

_____

Surname _____

Address _____

_____

_____ Postcode _____

Send this whole page to: Mills & Boon Book Club, Free Book Offer, FREEPOST NAT 10298, Richmond, TW9 1BR